I0531461

Brink of Life

Book 2: Brink of Life Trilogy

Rick Moskovitz

Illustration and design by Mary Verrandeaux

FLUKE TALE PRODUCTIONS

Brink of Life

Table of Contents

"...was I the same when I got up this morning? I almost think I can remember feeling a little different. But if I'm not the same, the next question is, Who in the world am I? Ah, that's the great puzzle!"

Alice's Adventures in Wonderland
Lewis Carroll

1

January 2059

SILENCE ENVELOPED HER. So many people and yet, this hushed stillness. And none more still than the strange man upon whose face she now gazed. Three fingers of her right hand were upon his cheek, which felt cold and waxen to her touch. She withdrew the hand and shuddered, then glanced at her arms, which were clothed in black. An arm gently draped across her shoulders. A brief stab of pain shot through the lower ribs on her left side, then another a couple of ribs higher next to her spine. She held her breath and the pain subsided. She kept her breathing shallow and the pain stayed at bay.

Now she glanced around the crowd. Tears fell from scattered faces. On a few other faces, though, she noticed ever so slight upturns at the corners of the mouths disturbing otherwise stolid expressions. Not everyone was here out of respect. The dead man before her must have had enemies. Were they also hers?

She heard the tempo of her pulse in both ears and her vision began to blur. Her breath quickened as the panic rose. The pain in her ribs caught her up short and she instinctively slowed her breathing to make it stop. Her vision cleared. The tension in her body subsided and a calm fell upon her as she observed the scene as if from far away. She focused all her attention on the drama unfolding before her, but could make no sense at all of any of it.

She was somehow at the center of this piece. Most eyes were upon her. Some faces wore expressions of concern, while on others she saw indifference and on still others glimmers of contempt.

"Who was this man?" she thought. "Who are these people? And how did I get here?"

Someone took her by the hand and led her out of the church as the pallbearers rolled the casket ahead of her.

"Watch your head, Mrs. Kresky," said a voice behind her as she ducked to slide into the backseat of the limo. By now, she realized she must be the widow.

She glanced in the rearview mirror, saw the face of another stranger and recoiled. This face belonged to her. And she was certain she had never seen it before.

2

SHE FELT THE LIMO RISE ever so slightly, then move silently forward on a cushion of air as it followed the hearse that bore the body of the man she presumed was her husband. The hearse passed through a bronze arch, then around a long curved driveway bordered by manicured grass that was punctuated by rows of identical bronze markers set flush with the ground. They were spaced just a few feet apart.

"Too close for bodies," she thought.

The hearse stopped in front of a one-story marble front building with a hip roof of thick, gray clay tiles and a huge double entry door of rippled glass, translucent, but obscure, teasing the imagination about what might lie within. The limo glided to a stop and settled gently to the ground.

The back of the hearse opened, and the casket was lifted to the ground and rolled to the entrance of the building. The doors slid apart to admit the building's newest client. As she watched the coffin roll through the opening, she couldn't help but think that a giant monster was about to swallow its prey. When she stepped out of the car, someone motioned her toward the building's entrance. She walked into the mouth of the monster as if in a dream.

Once within, she was faced with an enormous, gleaming cylindrical chamber, its length extending toward the far wall and its massive round door lying open toward her, revealing a brightly lit space inside. On the outside left surface of the chamber was a row of controls, a mixture of electronic interfaces and a large metal wheel designed to be turned by hand.

The pallbearers released a latch on the coffin and opened a panel on the end facing the chamber. They lifted the casket from the rear and the body slid into the chamber onto a platform that rolled it to the middle of the space within. A man in a snow-white jumpsuit turned the wheel. The door slowly slid shut. With an extended hiss, the chamber was sealed.

"Would you like the honors, Mrs. Kresky?" said the man in white.

She returned a bewildered look. What was she being asked to do? Somewhere in the thickly veiled recesses of her mind were images of funerals from long before her time when corpses were lowered into the ground and mourners took turns shoveling piles of earth onto the coffin's surface, a time-honored poetic ritual to say a final goodbye. Had this ritual evolved in the era of resomation to pushing the button that released the lye that would liquefy the loved one's earthly remains? Hardly poetic. And even less meaningful to her in the absence of any emotional connection to the body within. She shook her head to decline and turned to leave. As she crossed the threshold, she heard behind her the whir of an opening valve, followed by the tide of liquid rushing to consume its gruesome meal.

"What happens next?" she wondered as she stepped back into the limo.

"Where to, Mrs. Kresky?" asked the driver. The next move was up to her.

"Take me home." She had no idea where home was or what she would find when she got there, but it was time to find

4

out. She was now in control of her trajectory and she was flying blind.

The limo glided back under the arch, drove a mile or so through a wooded area, circled halfway around a quiet pond on which a lonely sailboat glided in lazy zig zags over the rippled surface, crossed a main thoroughfare and a sign with an arrow pointing right to "Boston 3 miles," and emerged into a neighborhood of well-kept homes, packed tightly side by side. From there it ascended a road that spiraled up a hill to another neighborhood of more elegant residences spaced with generous breathing room. Halfway up the hill was a stone front mansion behind a tall, iron fence. Chimneys at both ends of the house were capped with copper, the curves of each slope of the caps generously anointed with verdigris, attesting to the age of the building.

The car swung into the driveway and approached the massive gates, flanked by huge stone columns, then stopped. The driver glanced back at her.

"Do you have the remote," he asked.

She felt the panic return, punctuated by another stab of pain in her ribs. How long could she keep up the charade with so many obstacles and so many more likely to come? And yet, something told her that she couldn't let anyone know that she wasn't who she seemed to be. That would be more perilous. Perhaps even put her life at risk. The only thing she knew for sure was that she was lucky to be alive and wanted to continue breathing. How odd to have no history, no identity or connections with others, and still desperately cling to consciousness.

"Look in your bag, Mrs. Kresky," said the driver, pointing at the small clutch by her side. His voice brought her back to the present. She reached into the bag and felt around. At the bottom, she found only a thick metal tag, about an inch square. She pulled it out and held it up.

"That's it," said the driver. "Now open it, please." He gestured with his thumb and forefinger touching.

She followed his cue and grasped the tag firmly between her right thumb and forefinger. The gates swung open. She breathed a sigh of relief. One obstacle down. Now how would she get into the house? There was nothing else in the clutch that might serve as a key.

When they reached the front door and she emerged from the car, she quickly scanned the entry for signs of access. Just to the right of the door was a smooth black pad about the size of her hand. Above it was a tiny opening, perhaps large enough for a camera lens. She approached the door, placed her right hand flat against the pad and looked directly into the opening. She heard the snap of a lock and the door fell ajar. Another obstacle down. For the next challenges at least, she would enjoy a cloak of privacy.

"Will that be all, Mrs. Kresky?" came the driver's voice from behind her.

"Yes." She turned to face him. "Thank you so much for your patience. You can't imagine how difficult this day has been."

"Of course, Ma'am. I'm sorry for your loss." And he was gone. She was finally alone.

She stood in the cavernous foyer and wondered where to begin. This vast home must abound with clues about her identity and that of the dead man. She shuddered again as she remembered touching his cold, dead face upon first breaking into awareness. When she looked down at her widow's clothes, she felt a sudden urge to shed them and to wash the lingering residue of death from her body. Her investigation would begin in the bathroom, where she could examine the body she inhabited in detail.

She ascended the stairs and moved from room to room until she identified the master bedroom and the master bath. The bathroom was wholly lined in glass tile on every surface, including the floor and ceiling. Standing under the twelve foot ceiling she felt as though she were in a crystal palace, illuminated with multicolored lasers. While most of the surfaces were textured and obscure, one entire wall was mirrored. Clothed wholly in black within this palace, she resembled an evil queen.

Except for the brief glimpse in the rearview mirror of the limo, this was the first time she saw her face clearly and could linger on its features. It was a pretty face. Some might say exquisite. Her hair was jet black and straight, falling almost to her shoulders. A neat row of bangs was cut square about an inch above arching eyebrows that framed eyes that looked brown straight on, but with green and amber highlights that shone when viewed at an angle. She found this combination of hair and eye color exotic.

Her skin was the olive color of Middle Eastern lineage. Just beneath the eyes, she noticed a pale layer of texture that she wiped off to reveal a dark and slightly iridescent discoloration below her left eye. It was tender to her touch.

Her nose was straight, slender, and symmetrical, coming to a sharp point. A bit long by some standards, but adding a whisper of aristocracy to the overall impact of her visage. The smooth line of her upper lip formed a perfect cupid's bow. The lower lip was smooth and full, except for a tiny vertical scar interrupting the lower contour about an inch from the left corner. This was the only permanent blemish on an otherwise perfect face. She opened her mouth and smiled to examine her teeth, which were straight and white.

She drew back a step in order to take in the whole picture. Even after this close inspection, there wasn't a trace of familiarity. The face in the mirror remained a stranger.

Next she began stripping away the clothes. As they lay in a heap on the floor, she gazed at a body nearly as perfect as the face that accompanied it. It was slender with gentle curves at her hips and the rounded, firm breasts of a twenty-year-old. Could she really be so young? The dead man looked much older, at least forties, perhaps fifties.

A fading bruise covered her left lower ribs and when she turned her back to the mirror and looked over her shoulder, another brownish discoloration appeared over the attachment of her lowermost ribs to her spine. She inhaled deeply, expecting to feel the stabbing pain she'd felt at the funeral, but felt only a dull soreness at each site of injury. Who or what had inflicted these injuries? And did they have anything to do with how her husband had died?

In one corner of the room was a glass enclosed pod with a footprint only three feet square. A vertical array of nozzles graced each of the corner walls of the chamber. A touch screen by the door contained a pair of buttons. She stepped in and closed the door, held her breath and touched the first button. Short blasts of water shot from the sprays and stung her body from head to toe. Gentler bursts followed of a viscous liquid that formed a slick coating over her skin. The sensation was unexpectedly pleasant. She touched the second button, which released blasts of air from the nozzles that blew off the excess liquid, leaving her body feeling clean, dry, and silky smooth. She couldn't recall ever being washed in this manner before, but there was something very familiar about how her body felt when it was over.

In the bedroom closet hung a lavish wardrobe, including a range of lingerie from demure to radically obscene. She tried on a selection in front of the big bathroom mirror to jog her memory, but none of the images triggered any connections. Seeing herself in the raunchier outfits seemed particularly alien and distressing. And thinking of herself making love to the man in the coffin made her stomach turn. She settled on a pair of blue silk pajamas that felt warm and snug.

The day had been long and demanding. As much as she wanted answers to so many questions, she succumbed to drowsiness and collapsed on the bed, where she lay sound asleep until daybreak.

3

SUNLIGHT WAS STREAMING through the tall glass doors that nearly covered the east wall of the bedroom when she opened her eyes. She scanned the room to get her bearings, but nothing was familiar. She was still in someone else's house living someone else's life. If it was just a nightmare, she couldn't find a way to awaken from it.

She ran her fingers over the blue silk pajamas and found the sensation comforting. This feeling, at least, was familiar. Whoever she was, she had some knowledge of the world and had stored impressions of things within it and how they worked. Silk was delicate, smooth, and pleasing to the touch. One small thing of which she could be certain.

She stretched her arms above her head and swung her feet to the floor. She paused, aware that something was already missing from the night before. What was different? She brought her right hand to the lower ribs on the left side of her chest and pressed gently, then harder. The pain was gone. She turned and twisted in both directions. The pain in her back was also gone. When she pulled up her pajama top and looked for the bruise, there was no sign of it at all, just smooth, pink, pristine skin.

She walked into the bathroom and looked in the mirror. Gone also was the bruise beneath her left eye. She pulled on the skin beneath it and peered closely into the mirror. Nothing. Not a blemish. No tenderness to touch. Only the tiny scar on her lower lip still marred an otherwise perfect face, while a tiny lump the size of a pea in the indentation just behind her right earlobe was the only flaw in an otherwise perfect body.

Her stomach gurgled, accompanied by a gnawing sensation at the back of her throat, reminding her that she hadn't eaten anything since she'd first plunged into consciousness. Almost a day had passed since the funeral. Hunger, like the smoothness of silk, was another familiar sensation, although she had no idea what might appeal to her appetite. She descended the stairs and found her way into what seemed to be a kitchen, where she was surrounded by an unbroken expanse of metallic gray facing jutting out from three of the walls, interrupted only by a horizontal space with a glass counter dividing the façade on the far wall. When she rested her hand on the glass, a touch screen appeared, but the array of symbols seemed random and bewildering. Somewhere here must be food, but she had no inkling how to get it.

"Refrigerator," she muttered aloud, and an icon began glowing brightly on the screen. She touched it. The outline of a rectangle appeared on the cabinet face to her right and it slid toward the center of the room. On both sides of the module, shelves were illuminated, filled with an array of colorful liquids, compressed cubes of green, yellow, red and purple, covered glass bowls containing granular materials of various textures and colors, and tightly wrapped wedges of white and yellow, dark around the edges, and firm to the touch.

"Cheese," she guessed, withdrew one of the wedges and placed it on the counter. Something at least that she recognized. She selected a reddish orange container of liquid that she surmised was either vegetable or fruit juice. As hungry as she was, the variety of mysterious foods that lay before her was too overwhelming to choose among them. She touched the icon on the screen again and the module slid shut.

"Dishes." This time she spoke plainly. Another rectangle appeared, this time above the counter, and a cabinet slid open. She'd guessed right. The kitchen provided access to its contents in response to verbal commands. With the next command, she found knives and forks and tore into the block of cheese, which she devoured with gusto until her hunger was appeased. She washed it down with the juice, which was both salty and sweet in a pleasing combination that complemented the cheese. Hunger and thirst both slaked, she turned her attention back to deciphering her surroundings.

Back in the bedroom, she found few clues to her identity or that of her husband. There were no documents, no photographs, no clues to the occupations or activities of the occupants of this household. Except for the wardrobe in the closet and the round bed in the center of the room, there was a seamlessness to the room that echoed the seamlessness of the kitchen with its hidden cupboards and appliances.

As she moved through the house, she was struck by the austerity of the interior in stark contrast to the imposing and elegant exterior that she'd first seen the previous day. Furnishings were spare, like doll furniture, dwarfed by the enormous rooms that contained them. Expanses of gleaming polished floors spanned the distance between walls that appeared smooth and uniform around the perimeters of the rooms. It seemed as though nobody lived there. And yet, the closets in the bedroom were full of clothes and the kitchen was filled with food.

In the middle of the main floor was a rotunda, its ceiling rising several stories to its peak in the center of the room. In the center of the floor was a cylindrical tower, five feet tall and around a foot in diameter, capped with a shiny glass dome. A brilliant saber of blue light pierced the space from the base of the tower through the dome and all the way to the ceiling. When she passed her hand across the beam of light, the skin on the top of her hand glowed translucent blue, but nothing else happened. She'd imagined that this tower was a key that would reveal to her the house's secrets, but if it was, she had no idea how to engage it.

Next she found a brightly lit hallway with doors to a half dozen rooms, most of which were empty. In one of the rooms toward the end of the hall was what appeared to be a laboratory or perhaps an examination room. There was a cushioned table in the middle of the room and an array of electronic instruments on the white counters around its perimeter. Most astonishing, though, was a lifelike female figure standing in the far corner of the room, completely still.

"A mannequin," was her first impression. Then, from somewhere deep within the murky recesses of her memory came "SPUD," a vulgar term for advanced artificial intelligence entities, the term shortened from the archaic "sentient processing unit" and "sentient processing device." One of the many voids in her lost world was now peopled by these entities.

She approached the figure, which remained motionless, apparently unaware of her presence, and looked for a way to turn it on. The covering of her body under her clothing was seamless, without any buttons or compartments that might conceal controls. She backed away, regarding the figure at a distance, looking for clues. Then the lesson of the kitchen struck her and she tried a different strategy.

"Wake up!" she commanded. The figure stirred, met her gaze, and smiled.

"Good morning, Petra," said the SPUD. "It's so nice to see you again."

"Petra," she thought. "Now at least I have a name."

"And who are you?"

"Why I'm Brigid, of course, your personal medical attendant. Are you ready for an examination?" Brigid reached out her hands and gestured toward the examination table.

She hesitated a moment, considering the risk of putting herself in Brigid's hands, but saw an opportunity for learning more about herself. Still clad in the silk pajamas, she obediently lay face up on the table and awaited Brigid's next move. Brigid approached the table palms down and passed her hands over the length of Petra's body, barely brushing the surface. Then she bent close to her face and peered into each eye, a burst of orange light illuminating her own pupils with each look. She backed away and clasped her hands together.

"The examination is finished. You can get up now."

She obeyed, standing to face her examiner.

"So what did you find?" she asked.

"All your vital signs are normal...better than normal for your age." Brigid paused. "You are in remarkably sound health, considering your recent injuries."

"Injuries?"

"You sustained fractures of the left sixth rib anteriorly and the left ninth rib posteriorly as well as a fracture of your left zygomatic arch. You would know that as your 'cheekbone.'"

"When did that happen?"

"Three days ago."

"How?"

"I do not have that information. I only know what injuries occurred."

"Those sound like bad injuries. Why don't I still hurt?"

"They are almost fully healed. Another day and it will be as if they had never occurred."

"That doesn't sound normal."

"Normal? Not for most people. But for you, Petra, it's the usual matter of course. You possess extraordinary healing abilities."

"How can that be?"

"I don't have that information. I've been your personal medical attendant for the past three years. I've watched you recover from injuries during that time, but I have no knowledge of how you acquired that capacity."

"You said my vital signs were better than normal for my age...How old am I?"

Brigid's eyes opened wide. "You don't know how old you are?"

"I've just been through an event that's shaken me to my foundation. I'm feeling so confused."

"You were born on October 23, 2016."

"And today's date?" She held her breath in anticipation.

"Why it's January 9, 2059. You are 42 years old."

"How can that be?" she nearly shouted. "I don't look or feel a day over twenty."

"Twenty is your biological age," answered Brigid. "at least according to the length of the telomeres on your chromosomes. They have remained exactly the same length since I have been attending you. Your health is remarkable."

"But how?" she asked again.

"That information is not in my data banks."

She wondered whether Brigid could be trusted with the truth about her amnesia. Brigid was, after all, only a SPUD whose main purpose was to serve her. And she was her best shot for now at learning more about who she was.

"Brigid," she ventured, "could you help me with my memory?"

"What is the problem?"

"To be honest, I have no idea who I am. My memories go back less than a day. It was like I woke up in the middle of the funeral."

"What funeral? Has somebody died?"

"My husband. At least I think he was my husband. Did you also take care of him?"

"Yes, but he has not come to see me for weeks. I did not know that he had died. He was in excellent health."

"What about my memory?" said Petra, returning to the point. "Have I had some sort of head injury?"

Brigid approached her and placed the palms of both hands on the top of her head. She held them there for twenty seconds or so, then backed away.

"The blow to your face happened days ago, but did not apparently injure your brain. There has been no other head trauma, but...there has been an anomaly...a singularity in the pattern of your brainwaves. I have records of your brainwaves over the time I've attended you. These patterns are like a signature or a fingerprint. There is an underlying order that stays constant for any given person. Your pattern has completely changed as if you became someone else altogether. That's impossible, of course."

Impossible, perhaps. But that was exactly what it felt like to her...like she was a visitor in a body that belonged to someone else, someone whose life, except for the clues that she'd been able to gather in the house and from Brigid, was a total mystery to her. How did she get there? And what became of the person whose body she now inhabited.

As curious as she was to learn more about Petra Kresky, into whose life she'd so abruptly plunged, she was all the more intent upon discovering who she'd been and what had happened to her before she'd made the improbable leap from her own body to this one. Or did she even have a personal history? Perhaps, like Brigid, her consciousness had been digitally designed, fully formed and ready to merge with a physical entity. But unlike Brigid, that entity wasn't made of silicone and carbon fiber, but of flesh and blood...and not created from scratch, but stolen from another human being.

4

SOMETHING EXTRAORDINARY was happening to her body. She seemed to possess the capacity to heal from severe injuries in a matter of hours. She would put it to the test.

She returned to the kitchen where she found a set of ceramic knives with finely honed zirconium blades. She selected a knife with a three-inch blade, placed the edge against the inside of her left wrist, pressed it against the flesh and drew the sharp edge across its breadth. The skin parted, wept drops of blood, then opened wider, gushing bright red blood in pulsating spurts. Her head swam momentarily as she watched the blood flow, but her vision returned with a clarity and vibrancy that felt almost supernatural. The split-second pain of the incision was followed by the warmth of blood pouring from the wound over her flesh. She felt intensely alive.

She watched with fascination at the flow of blood for a dozen seconds before instinctively pressing her free hand over the wound to stop it. She pressed hard for half a minute and released the pressure. The bleeding had nearly stopped despite the quarter inch gap between the edges of the wound.

Suddenly, the scene around her faded and she stood beside a sliding glass door with a dagger lunging at her face. She parried with her left forearm, which bore the brunt of the blow and turned red with blood. Her right foot shot at her assailant's groin and he went down, dislodging the knife from his hand. She grabbed his head with both hands, twisting sharply. She heard a crunch. His body stilled. Out of the corner of her eye she saw reflected in the glass luxuriant red hair set off by porcelain white skin. As she turned to get a better look at the reflection, the scene again shifted and she was back in the present staring at the gash in her wrist, now bloodless.

As she pondered the scene that had just flashed through her mind, she wondered about this woman's ability to defend herself so deftly, but wondered even more about her willingness to kill without mercy. She moved like a spy...or an assassin. On which side of the law did she stand? And when she imagined the face reflected in the glass, one thing felt certain. She knew that face. It belonged to her.

5

"THE TOWER," she thought upon awakening the next morning. She pictured the projection from the floor of the rotunda with the blue light piercing the space above it. "There has to be a way to unlock it."

She descended the stairs and made her way to the cavernous space in the center of the house. As she approached the structure at its center, she scanned it carefully for any detail she may have missed. Its body was solid stone, perfectly round and polished to a high gloss. The glass dome was also symmetrical and smooth. Around the beam of blue light emitting from the center of the column was a seemingly bottomless darkness.

She placed the palms of her hands on opposite sides of the dome. Nothing happened. As she stared into the darkness, she remembered that other things in this house had responded to the sound of her voice. She backed away from the device.

"System on," she commanded.

The blue light rippled momentarily. The tower slid downward until the top of the dome was flush with the floor. The light rearranged itself in the space before her until a colorful array of rotating icons danced before her eyes. At the center was a spherical stylized letter G, slightly larger than the other symbols, randomly spinning and progressing through a rainbow of colors. She recognized it and reached out to touch it with a forefinger. The shapes dissolved, replaced first by what seemed like a bottomless void, then a single icon, this time of an old-fashioned microphone.

"Who is Arlo Kresky?" She asked aloud.

The space before her once more dissolved to black before a human figure materialized within it. At first it shimmered in transparent fragments, then gradually filled in until it appeared solid and substantial. The face belonged to a man of around thirty...clean shaven...gray eyes and swarthy skin...his mouth in a straight line...serious, humorless, verging on grim. He stood around six feet tall, slim, but tightly built, with well-defined muscles accentuated by form-fitting clothes. Something about him was familiar, although she felt certain she'd never seen this image before.

The man in the coffin came to mind. The figure before her appeared vital and full of color in contrast to the waxen face of the dead man. And it was younger by at least 20 years. But as she examined it closely, she became convinced that it was the same man, Arlo Kresky, in a younger incarnation. And this man seemed to be making eye contact with her.

"Talk to me," she demanded. The face turned slightly upward and the hands rose to waist height. It seemed to be coming to life.

"Whoever you are, you now have the privilege of gazing upon my life's ambition. And if you are seeing this, then I may already be dead."

She inferred that this was a one-way conversation. Aside from responding to verbal prompts, the figure before her seemed unaware of her identity or even of her presence. She tested her theory by walking around him. Neither his eyes nor his body followed her movements.

She reached out to touch his arm. The space beneath her fingers deformed to her touch and she felt it push back. The spongy sensation felt neither solid nor the consistency of flesh. There was only a sense of some nondescript substance giving way and springing back when she removed the pressure. Action and reaction. Nothing more.

"My dream has been immortality," Kresky continued, "but there have been so many obstacles. Not the least of these has been the limited resources of our planet. With ten billion people already and widespread starvation, the world has resisted any technology that threatened to further stretch its resources.

"I devoted my wealth to this quest, enlisting the best minds in cybernetics, biology, and quantum computing to design a new host for our consciousness after we died. While there have been whispers of others creating human hosts for the dead, society has rejected such a solution on both moral and environmental grounds."

She was by now deeply engrossed in his story. Something about it resonated within her.

"We considered becoming avatars in virtual worlds. But as realistic as such worlds can feel, they are no substitute for continuing to live in the world we know. Then came the idea of a real-world avatar: a virtual body that could interact physically with reality. It could be eternally young, invulnerable to harm, and sparing on its demands on our resources. Except for the renewable power that animated it, it would require no food, no sustenance of any kind. And it would create no waste. The perfect human being."

She looked again into the pale gray eyes and felt herself shudder. Something about those eyes evoked a deep sense of horror, belied by the dispassionate discourse that spilled from his mouth.

"You are looking at the fourth iteration of the corporeal avatar. I am imbued with some of the characteristics of Arlo Kresky and can tell you about him, but I lack his consciousness or, for that matter, any consciousness. We've solved part of the physical problem, but not the essential goal of integrating body with mind. And I am tethered to this place by this machine. We have not yet figured out how to let me roam freely in this world."

So now she had some idea of her dead husband's passion, but she still had little idea who he was. The only clue to that was the involuntary shudder that warned her of something sinister. She'd had enough of his presence for now.

"Close portal," she commanded, remembering more about how such systems functioned. The figure disintegrated and faded again to black.

"How did Arlo Kresky die?" she asked next.

This time her words evoked an old-fashioned hologram of a flawless young woman with flowing blond hair and too symmetrical features.

"Arlo Kresky was found dead in bed by his wife Petra on January 7. Rescue personnel were unable to revive him. Although Mr. Kresky was a fitness fanatic and believed to be in exceptional health, investigators found no evidence of foul play. Tissue samples were taken at the scene. His body was released for resomation without an autopsy."

Why would an apparently healthy man suddenly die? Medical care at his level of access should have detected any signs of heart disease or other threats to survival years in advance. It didn't add up.

"Did Kresky have any known enemies?" she asked.

The holographic reporter faded away and in her place appeared the busts of a half dozen people, mostly men. She startled upon seeing her own face at the end of the row.

"Here are some people who may have borne malice toward Arlo Kresky," said a disembodied voice.

"What about her?" she asked, pointing at her own image. "Why her?"

"Kresky was known to be a jealous man with a violent temper. There have been rumors that his wife Petra was a victim of it. She sustained unexplained injuries over the years, perhaps as recently as a day or two before his death."

"And the others?"

"Former friends, business associates, people he's been accused of cheating or threatening."

She had enough new information for one day. She waved her arm and the images faded away, replaced by the array of icons.

"Shut down," she commanded, and the icons dissolved to black. The floor rumbled. The top of the tower rose until it was back to its full five feet of height. The blue beam shot out from the center of the glass dome to pierce the space above it. The ghost of Arlo Kresky was back in hiding within his machine, reduced to a string of zeros and ones until she chose to summon it again.

6

"TAP, TAP, TAP." The sound was coming from somewhere on the ground floor. "Tap, tap, tap." The rhythm was deliberate. The series of taps came at regular intervals, separated by half a minute.

She descended from the bedroom and moved softly around the perimeter of the house, listening. "Tap, tap, tap.' Now louder as she approached the kitchen. Upon entering the kitchen, she noticed a service door she hadn't seen before that opened to the side of the house. The tapping got louder and more insistent. She walked to the door.

"Who's there?" she demanded.

"Connor." The answer was unhelpful. The name meant nothing to her.

"Petra, it's Connor," the voice insisted. "Please let me in."

So at least he knew her. And he was addressing her with a familiarity that implied friend, not foe. He could be another clue to her identity. She considered the risk, then commanded the door to open. She heard a deadbolt slide and the door swung open. A young man rushed inside and gestured for her to close it.

Connor appeared in his early twenties, around the same as her biological age. Six feet tall and slender, but muscular, he had sculpted features, blond hair, and blue eyes.

"Gorgeous," she caught herself thinking, then felt something peculiar about her reaction. Why shouldn't she find this man attractive?

"Thank God you're safe," Connor said and moved in to embrace her. She instinctively backed away and he stopped short.

"Why didn't you come in the front?" she asked.

"The surveillance," he replied. "I don't think it's safe for us to be seen together right now."

"Why not?" she thought, but deemed it prudent not to ask. She was not ready to expose her ignorance or her vulnerability to this man.

"Some questions have been raised about Arlo's death," Connor said, answering her unspoken question. "If people knew about us, we might come under suspicion. And I no longer have a legitimate reason to be here now that he's dead."

"So we're lovers?" she thought and found the idea oddly delicious. She regretted for a moment fending off his embrace. She relaxed her posture to appear less defensive. The maneuver had the desired effect.

Connor approached her again, placed his hands on her shoulders, and brought his face close enough to hers that she could feel his breath. She moved into the kiss. His lips were soft and moist. She was lost in his embrace, feeling her whole body responding to his touch. Yes, they must be lovers. And yet...again something off about her response...like she'd never been with him before...or perhaps with any man.

The kiss was deep and lingering. When it was over, she found herself staring into the azure blue of his eyes. She wondered whether she'd been in love with him. Something told her, at least, that she could trust him.

He stared back with a probing gaze that hinted that he, too, was puzzled about their interaction. How could he fail to notice her bewilderment? Or was there something else he was trying to understand?

"Where have you been?" she asked next, fishing for more clues. "I missed you at the funeral." She would certainly have noticed this man had he been there.

"Lying low at home, working on the biography," Connor replied. "I'm still planning to finish it. People will want to know about him more than ever. Dead celebrities make good copy. I couldn't come to the funeral. If people saw us looking at each other, they might have gotten ideas."

More clues. Definitely lovers. Definitely secret. Connor was a writer, a biographer, and Arlo Kresky was his project.

Connor reached out, caressed her cheek, and began to move in for another embrace. She backed away. Enough for one day. She needed time to process what had already transpired between them.

"I'm exhausted," she said. "It's been a long day. Will you come back again tomorrow?"

"Of course, but I'd rather stay."

"I know, but I need some time. So much has happened. I need time to figure some things out. How can I reach you?"

"The usual way." That was no help at all.

"You mean...?"

"The private channel." Still no help. "Never mind. I'll find you." And he was out the door.

Now what? Some answers, but far more new questions. She'd been married to Arlo Kresky. Connor was his biographer and apparently her lover. How long had they been seeing each other? And how had their affair begun? Did the affair have anything to do with the beating she'd apparently taken around the time of her husband's death? Did it have anything to do with her husband's demise? Had she killed him? Had Connor? Had they planned it together? Or was this a blind alley with neither of them involved?

Unless more pieces to the puzzle fell into place soon, Connor would discover that she didn't remember him or anything else about her life before the last couple of days.

7

THE GASH IN HER WRIST healed with a speed resembling time-lapse photography. It closed completely within four hours, the scar fading and vanishing entirely by the next morning. No pain or sensation lingered to hint at the gaping wound that was present just hours before. The test was a success. She wasn't entirely invulnerable to harm, but her body possessed an astounding capacity to repair itself.

Even more fantastic was the portal into her past that opened in response to the self-inflicted injury. That together with the momentary euphoria that accompanied the act tempted her to repeat it. She wondered whether the effects, if they recurred at all, would be proportional to the severity of injury.

She grasped the ceramic knife again with her right hand and gazed upon it. Knives of this kind had been around for decades, almost entirely replacing the traditional steel implements that predated them. Made from zirconium oxide, they were nearly as hard as diamonds and were honed to a sharpness that produced clean incisions in whatever material they pierced. The ease with which she could plunge it into her body sent a shiver down her spine. Her hand trembled a moment. Then she slipped it back into its place in the kitchen compartment.

But she couldn't get the thought out of her head of cutting herself again. It was there when she awoke in the morning and persisted like an itch that needed scratching. Two days after the first experiment, she drew the knife again from its storage place, held the handle this time in both hands at arm's length, and plunged it to the hilt into her belly. The pain this time was agonizing and the blood flow copious.

"What have I done?" she wondered. "Am I going to die?" She had no idea what organs she'd pierced or what might be the consequences.

She began to black out. When her vision cleared, a woman was sitting by her side, pressing both hands firmly on the gaping wound in her abdomen. She placed her own hands on top of the other woman's and felt comforted by the contact. She saw in her face a mixture of concern and affection. The woman smiled softly, then brought her face to hers and kissed her gently on the lips. Her touch felt familiar. And when she rose from the kiss and the light played upon her face, the face was also familiar.

"Macklyn." The name came silently to her lips. And in place of the pain in her belly was a stirring between her legs and a longing that made little sense in the midst of a catastrophe. Macklyn's right hand slid tenderly down her belly and over her soft mound. Her touch was now all she could feel. She closed her eyes in ecstasy. When she opened them again, she was alone.

Blood was everywhere. So much blood. She had no idea there was that much blood in her body. In the middle of her belly was a vertical gash three inches long and an inch wide. But the only place that wasn't bloody was the space within the margins of the wound. It was as though the wound had sucked backed all the blood within it and had cauterized the bleeders. And there were no bits of organ or fecal matter. Only pink, clean flesh along the margins and into its depths.

"Macklyn." The name came to her lips. She repeated it over and over to commit it to memory. "Macklyn." Who was she and why was she there? Was this all just a hallucination or was it a memory of Macklyn coming to rescue her from a long past injury?

More mysterious were the feelings of arousal that were now magnified in her recollection of the encounter. As far as she could tell, she was not attracted to women. She imagined herself sexually with men...at least in her current incarnation. But Macklyn's presence was both deeply comforting and intensely erotic. Another piece of a puzzle that so far made little sense at all.

When she arose from the floor of the kitchen, puddles of crimson and maroon outlined an unsullied space in the shape of her torso. She ascended the stairs to the master bath, where she stepped into the cleansing pod to wash away the remnants of her self-inflicted carnage. There remained the inch-wide gap between the edges of her wound. Even with her remarkable healing powers, she decided it would be prudent to approximate the edges of the wound in order to minimize scarring.

She considered returning to Brigid for help, but wasn't ready to explain how the wound had occurred. Searching the bathroom, she discovered an extensive stash of first aid materials, perhaps attesting to the frequency of injuries she'd suffered at the hands of her husband. She selected a roll of clear, elasticized material, several inches wide, and wrapped it in overlapping layers around her belly, bringing the edges of the wound neatly together.

The horror of what she'd done washed back over her. The impulse had been overwhelming. But even with this resilient body, it had only been a matter of luck that the injury didn't prove fatal. So many organs and blood vessels had been in the path of the knife. A fraction of an inch one way or another was all it might have taken to end her life. The gamble had paid off handsomely in terms of the window it had opened into her past, but she couldn't afford ever to gamble like that again. She'd need to find safer ways to peer across the divide between her new life and her old one.

And then there was Connor. She wasn't ready to let him in on the secret of her remarkable body or the mystery of how she came to occupy it. If she were ever to expose her body to his gaze or to his touch, it would have to wait until all evidence of her moment of madness had vanished.

8

THE PAIN THAT SHOT through the base of her skull felt as though it was searing her brain. She sat bolt upright and pressed the fingers of both hands against the muscle insertions on the ridges of her skull. This maneuver failed to dampen the pain. She tried to stand, but staggered and fell back onto the bed. Was she having a stroke? Could she be dying?

Then for just a moment or two bells rang inside her head, sounding as loud as the pain was intense. One stroke, like the bells in a church tower, then silence...and the pain was gone. She reached in her mind for the sound of the bells, grasping at something familiar yet elusive. She heard the aftertones resonate, then fade to oblivion.

She rose again from the bed. This time, she was steady and made her way to the bathroom. She examined herself in the mirror, but found nothing amiss. Her pupils were equal and normal in size. There were no signs of injury to her head or face. Her eyes weren't even bloodshot. What was happening to her? And was it going to happen again?

She considered finding a doctor, but had no idea what risk that might entail. She wasn't prepared to explain the abdominal wound from the previous day, which was already closing nicely, but still visible. Then she thought of Brigid and made her way down the corridor to the examining room.

"Wake up, Brigid," she commanded as she entered the room. Brigid sprang to attention.

"Good morning, Petra," she said.

"Good morning Brigid. Something frightening just happened to me and I need your opinion."

"What seems to be the problem?"

"I awoke this morning with a pain in the back of my head...the worst pain of my life...at least the worst I can imagine. It felt like I'd been shot."

Brigid approached her and placed both hands around her head. Her fingers made their way over every inch of her skull. Then she backed away.

"Well?"

"There is no sign of injury," said Brigid. "But the blood flow in your brain appears increased as if it were reacting to some sort of shock."

"Like what?"

"I have insufficient experience with this pattern. I can only tell that the shock must have been severe."

She wondered whether her nervous system could be registering a delayed reaction to the self-inflicted abdominal wound, or perhaps to the emotional shock of the memory it had evoked. Then there were the bells. Could they be a clue to an event not yet recovered from the life she'd left behind?

Her attention turned for now to learning more about the life she'd begun to live. It was time to venture beyond the confines of Petra's house into the surrounding community. She left on foot, descending the steep hill on which the mansion perched until she reached level ground and a well-trafficked street, then headed toward a swell of pedestrians that seemed to indicate a commercial district.

She walked down the street looking for anything familiar. There was nothing that suggested that she'd ever been here before. The sidewalks were crowded with unfamiliar faces of people that jostled her as they passed.

Then at around twenty paces, she spotted an exotic looking young man with silky looking dark skin, finely sculpted features, and piercing blue eyes that angled slightly upward at the corners. As he headed toward her, she sensed that she'd seen him before. But where...and when? He bumped her as he passed and melted into the crowd.

When she returned home, she found a tiny cylinder, not much bigger than a needle, tucked into the waistband of her pants. It was transparent and devoid of any markings that might provide clues to its purpose. From the recesses of her mind, however, she recognized it as a memory module, the kind that interfaced with cybernetic enhancements of human intelligence.

She stripped naked and stood before the mirror, searching for anomalies in the continuity of her skin. She was about to give up when she spotted the tiny mole just beneath the crease above her left thigh. It was only a millimeter in diameter and had a slightly bluish hue. She dug the fingernail of her right forefinger at the edge of the mole. It flipped up, revealing a tiny cavity in her skin. She carefully slid the cylinder into the opening and it went in easily all the way to its hilt. She brushed her finger over the mole and it snapped back into place.

What now? She could not remember how to activate the module. And she had no idea why the familiar stranger might have passed it to her or whether he was friend or foe. Installing the module in her body was a colossal risk. She could lose whatever remnants of memory she'd already recovered or her thoughts could become hopelessly scrambled.

Later that night, slipping into the twilight state of sleep when dreamlike images sometimes intrude into consciousness and merge with the real world's landscape, the walls of her bedroom shrank and closed around her until she found herself in a much smaller room. Sickly green paint on the walls was peeling in some places. Other patches of wall were down to bare plaster. In place of the vastness of the bedroom in which she'd gone to bed, the ceiling was now only seven or eight feet high, the bed only wide enough for one person and long enough for a child. She turned onto her stomach to keep the lumpy bed from poking at her ribs. A musty odor infiltrated her nostrils, at the same time both familiar and strange.

A door slammed in an adjacent room. Heavy footsteps lumbered across a creaky floor, then stopped well short of the door to her room. She swung her feet onto the floor and, still barefoot, rose from the bed and tiptoed to the door. When she opened it a crack and peered out, she saw him sitting hunched over the wooden table, one hand around a bottle and the other around a glass half filled with an amber liquid. A matted rim of graying hair surrounded a balding dome save for a stray forelock that glistened with sweat and dove down his forehead to the bridge of his nose. His eyes squinted in the fading light and his mouth contorted in a grimace.

She watched him toss back the drink and waited. After a minute or two, his face relaxed. He sighed deeply. Then his shoulders relaxed and fell. Like the musty odor, this scene too was both familiar and strange. The sight of this grizzled man evoked a mixture of affection and fear. He was someone important in her life. Her father? Her grandfather?

Her chest thumped with the beat of her heart and she instinctively brought her right hand to her breast to quiet it. Her palm found the flat chest of a child beneath a ragged ribbed men's undershirt she was wearing as a nightgown. When she glanced down, she saw that it came below her knees. She suddenly felt tiny and vulnerable.

Then out of the blue from within the terror in her heart came an impulse to approach this man, to touch him and to hear his voice. She felt herself open the door and felt the bare pads of her feet move across the wooden floor. As she got closer, the combined smell of the liquor and stale sweat almost overwhelmed her, but she pressed on until she was standing beside him just to his left. He stared straight ahead, apparently unaware of her presence.

"Papa?" she whispered in a tiny child's voice that she somehow knew as her own.

His head turned slowly in her direction. Then his left arm lashed backward and sent her sprawling across the floor. Her face stung from the blow. Her tongue licked at the blood dripping from a gash on her left lower lip. Her elbows and knees bore the brunt of the impact with the floor. But the pain that this man inflicted yet again upon her heart was the most poignant and lasting of this encounter.

"You're supposed to be in bed, Petra," he growled, looking back at her over his shoulder and raising his arm again as if ready to deliver another blow. His emphasis on the first syllable of her name bore an extra measure of contempt. "Get the hell back in your room where you belong!"

She cowered under his gaze, then turned onto her hands and knees and crawled around the table out of range. He raised his arm again and jerked it back in a threatening manner, but he was by now too drunk to get out of his chair. She sniveled as she made her way back to her room. Once there, she closed the door behind her, stood up and reached for the lock to fasten it, but the hasp hung limply from a single screw. It had long since been broken in one of her father's drunken rages. By the time she was back in the child sized bed, she was beginning to feel at home in this child's body, accompanied by an awareness that the scene she'd just experienced had been played out time and again in countless variations, most of which ended the same.

As she cried herself to sleep, she felt the bed shift beneath her body. The walls again began to move and the ceiling rose. When she fully opened her eyes, she was back in the vast bedroom and oversized bed of the adult Petra's mansion. She lay staring at the ceiling and contemplated what she'd just experienced. It felt too real to have been a dream, especially the pain of the blow. It had felt as though she were experiencing these events in real time. She remembered the memory module that she'd plugged into her body that afternoon. Perhaps it contained the lost memories of the body she inhabited. What she'd just experienced might have been a virtual replay of a childhood experience. Intensely familiar and at the same time oddly alien. Petra's childhood...and yet, she did not feel like Petra. Even the name felt like something outside of herself.

9

THE NEXT MORNING, she headed back to the examination room to find Brigid.

"Wake up, Brigid," she commanded. The SPUD came to life.

"Good morning, Petra," Brigid said, "It's good to see you again. What can I do for you?"

She stripped off her pants to expose the mole at the top of her right thigh. She flipped it open with her fingernail and pressed on the flesh around it to expose the tip of the cylinder. She extracted it and held it out to Brigid.

"Do you know what this is?" she asked.

"Yes. It's a data stick. It contains input for your onboard cortical prosthesis. You would experience it as memory."

"Can you tell me how to access this memory?"

"Once installed, it works much like your native memory. You can think about an event and the details will come to mind. Remembering a birthday, for example."

"And what if I can't remember anything at all? What if there are no markers in my memory for events?"

"In that case, the memories might appear at random, triggered by perceptions and sensations in the present that are connected with them in some way."

"I need more order than that. I have to piece together my history, to know who I am."

"Sometimes, thinking about a specific date or place can connect with a memory," Brigid offered, "and sometimes thinking about a person."

As she drifted off to sleep that night, she imagined the face of the swarthy young man she'd seen on the street, who she believed had passed her the memory module. A name formed on her lips.

"Ethan," she spoke half aloud. Then she was in an alley, late at night, with only a sliver of moonlight intruding upon the shadows around her. She shivered under the thin wrap that covered the skimpy costume she'd worn that night to perform. She shuddered as she remembered the feeling of groping hands pulling at her tiny G-string as she writhed to the music. Now on the street, her body was shielded from the humiliation of leering gazes, but she still felt vulnerable and exposed.

Suddenly she sensed that she was being followed. She whirled around to find herself face to face with the striking young man she'd pictured on the brink of slumber. He was dressed in a form-fitting white jumpsuit that emphasized his sinewy body and didn't resemble any of the customers in front of whom she'd just disgraced herself.

"Hello, Petra," he said.

"How did you know my name?"

"I've been observing you for some time. I have a proposition for you that I think you'll find attractive."

"So he's just like the others, after all," she thought, pulling her wrap closer around her, and began to walk away.

"How would you like to reclaim control of your body...and your dignity?" he continued.

She stopped again and turned to face him. If this was a come-on, it was at least very different from what she'd come to expect.

"I'm listening."

"Please hear me out before you judge," he went on. "What I'm about to tell you may shock you at first, but once you've had time to consider it, I think you'll change your mind."

He told her that he represented a few wealthy and powerful clients who were willing to pay huge sums for a shot at immortality. Part of fulfilling that dream meant finding healthy young bodies for them to inhabit after they died. His organization had advanced the science of migrating consciousness to the point that consciousness could be exchanged between bodies.

"So you're asking me to give up my body? To die in place of someone else?"

"Yes. That's exactly what I'm asking. But it's not likely to happen for a very long time. And with fifty million dollars, the time you have left could be lived in vastly better circumstances than your life today."

"But I'll age, too. So what's the advantage for someone else of having my body?"

"That's the other part of the deal. Your benefactor will want a young healthy body. So we'll arrange for you to have the Ambrosia Conversion, a genetic process that will prevent your body from aging further. In addition to becoming fabulously wealthy, you'll also be eternally young and healthy."

"Eternally...you mean as long as I get to live."

"For you, that may mean a very long time indeed. Your benefactor is herself young and healthy and she's had the Conversion. She could live indefinitely. Her contract has been provided by her employer as an insurance policy against accidental death."

Ethan gave her twenty-four hours to make up her mind. It took her only minutes to decide. Accepting his proposal would mean never having to degrade herself again like she'd done that night and so many other nights before. She had little to lose and might even wind up living longer than if she'd lived out her natural life.

The street scene faded, and she was lying on a stretcher, a needle in her arm attached by plastic tubing to a transparent bag hanging on a pole. Ethan stood beside her, explaining the procedure. The IV bag contained an infusion of nanoparticles that would map her brain to the cloud via a tiny transmitter implanted in the hollow behind her right ear. That would become the portal through which her unknown benefactor...buyer...might someday jump into her brain. She should have felt imperiled, but by the time it was over, she felt exhilarated by the combination of risk and invulnerability. She would never grow old and feeble. The world would be her playground.

When she awoke the next morning, she wasn't sure whether the visions of the night before had been memories or just a dream. It all seemed preposterous...transferring consciousness between bodies, eternal youth. And yet, it made sense of so many things that didn't fit together in any other script.

Just suppose that the contract was real and that its final conditions had been fulfilled. What if she were the person on the other side of the contract now living in Petra's body? That would explain her absence of memories of Petra's life, memories that Ethan had endeavored to prompt with the module containing Petra's memories. And it would explain her sense of alienation from her body and her lack of recognition of Petra's face as her own.

But why then wouldn't she remember anything of her former life? Why had she come to her new existence like a newborn with a memory like a blank slate? Who was she and would she ever reclaim her real identity, or was she destined to remain Petra Kresky forever?

10

THE IMAGE OF MACKLYN comforting her and caressing her haunted her. She visualized the face that was now etched sharply into her memory. Oval face, coffee colored skin with scattered freckles over her cheekbones and across the bridge of her nose, short black hair that framed her face with soft curls, and full, soft lips turned up in a gentle smile that radiated warmth and reassurance. And as she continued to envision her face, a new feeling rose within her. She missed this mysterious stranger. She longed to be with her again.

"Macklyn." She repeated the name like a mantra. "Will I have to cut myself again to see you?" Her temptation to repeat that brutal self-mutilation was tempered by the memory of all the blood and the realization of how close she might have come to dying. Even those wounds had healed with remarkable speed. The margins of the gash had closed within a couple of days and no trace remained by the end of the third day.

In the days following that vision, headaches occurred with increasing frequency, stabbing pains at the base of her skull that seemed to penetrate all the way to her eyes. Sometimes the pain was accompanied by bells, other times by the sound of gunshots. And once she heard a shouted word that she struggled vainly to make out.

Following the vision of Macklyn, Connor had returned and had infiltrated her thoughts, her heart, and her bed. Being

44

with him was both wonderful and bewildering. She loved the sensation of being filled with him. The rhythm of him moving inside her reverberated throughout her body in exquisite harmony. His lips and tongue brought her to peaks of arousal and delight. And yet, lingering in the back of her mind was Macklyn. And for a few moments at a time it would be Macklyn's lips on her nipples and Macklyn's tongue exploring her mouth.

"You look a million miles away, Petra," Connor said as they sipped wine one evening after making love. "Where are your thoughts?"

"I was wondering about someone I once knew," she said.

"Another man? A long lost love?" he teased.

"A woman...a friend," she said, "from very long ago. Another life."

"It couldn't have been so long ago. How old are you? Twenty-two? Twenty-three?"

"Well, it feels like long ago." She laughed, avoiding his question. "When you're young, time goes by so slowly."

"What happened to your friend?"

"I have no idea. We went our separate ways and I've lost track of her entirely. I honestly wouldn't know where to look."

Connor reached over and put his hand on her thigh. She warmed to his touch and leaned in to a kiss. When she closed her eyes, she imagined she was kissing the velvety lips of another woman.

What was most remarkable is that while Connor was present and substantial, she could not be certain that Macklyn was even real or had ever existed. But in her mind's eye, she was every bit as real and as much a part of her life and

45

personal history as Connor or Arlo Kresky. Perhaps even more.

As she drifted off to sleep that night after Connor left, she lingered on the feeling of that last kiss, but it was Macklyn's touch she imagined and Macklyn's face she saw before her as she opened her eyes.

Then the room faded away and she was sitting at a bar, an empty martini glass on the counter in front of her. Her head was swimming. The lights were all surrounded by yellow halos. When she tried to stand, her legs, exposed below too snug shorts, were too wobbly to hold her and she settled back onto the barstool. In the mirror behind the bar, she saw the wispy figure of a teenager wearing a halter top, her hair tied back in a ponytail.

A hand crept across the exposed skin of her left thigh and fingers slid under the edge of her shorts. When she turned, a middle-aged man was sitting next to her, leering. She could smell the whiskey on his breath and the stink of old sweat.

"Time for us to go," he said, pulling her up roughly from the stool and moving his hand from her thigh to her buttocks to keep her on her feet. She was too helpless from whatever he'd put in her drink to resist. They headed for the door.

As he pulled the door open, an arm shot out and grabbed it by the edge, blocking its path. It was a woman's arm, slender, but powerful. The man turned toward the intruder and laughed, then demanded that she let go of the door. She held fast. He removed his hand from the door and gave her a shove. The woman caught him by the arm and in a single sharp motion broke it, forcing him to the floor. Then she took his victim by the hand and led her to safety.

When she next opened her eyes, someone was sitting vigil by her bedside. As her vision cleared, she made out the features of a woman in her early twenties, slender and fit, with coffee colored skin, delicate features, and a sprinkling of freckles across the bridge of her nose.

"You're safe here," said the woman in a gravelly voice, patting her hand. "He's gone. He can't hurt you now."

"What happened to me?" she asked.

"You were drugged. He put something in your drink and was planning to rape you. But he won't be hurting anyone for quite some time." She paused, then met her gaze. "I'm Macklyn."

"I'm…" she began. "I'm not entirely sure who I am." She shook her head. "Thank you for saving me. How did you learn how to do that?"

"Years of training. You could learn to do that, too. If you let me teach you, you won't ever have to be a victim again."

When she awoke the next morning, the scenes from her vision were still fresh and some of what followed intruded into her consciousness.

"Macklyn," she thought. "Younger and slimmer than the woman I saw before, but the same calming presence. So this is how we met."

Macklyn was a highly skilled covert operative for a government agency. She'd recruited her into the agency, becoming her mentor, then her handler. She'd been an apt pupil, soon exceeding her teacher's skills. And along the way, despite all the rules of their trade, they became lovers.

But even as these details filtered into her awareness, one crucial piece of information eluded her. She still didn't know her own name.

11

NOW THAT SHE HAD a visual impression of Arlo Kresky, she grasped the opportunity to evoke Petra's memories of him. Since her previous virtual experiences arose during the twilight state of sleep, she concluded that detaching her focus from current reality was a necessary condition for permitting the inflow of images from the past. Drowsiness was one way to achieve that. Meditation might be another, perhaps more controllable approach.

She sat quietly and focused her attention on the rhythm of her breathing. As she felt her body and mind begin to relax, she allowed the image of Kresky from the hologram to materialize in her mind's eye. When her attention drifted, she brought it back to the image, coupled with the rhythm of her breathing. She lost track of time, and then the room around her faded away.

Now she was sitting on a tufted leather sofa facing a large mahogany desk with an empty high-backed chair behind it. A tall, muscular man who appeared to be in his thirties was half-sitting on the leading edge of the desk, looking down at her. His expression was severe. She could feel her body trembling.

"What could you be thinking, coming here?" said Arlo Kresky. "Are you expecting charity?" he added with a sneer.

The trembling intensified. She could find no words and just sat helplessly, avoiding his gaze.

"Do you have any idea how much you owe me?" he asked, standing and advancing toward her until he towered over her.

As tiny as she felt, she tried to make herself even smaller, but could not become invisible.

"Three and a half million," she stammered at last, "but it might as well be ten times that for all the chance I have of ever being able to pay it back."

Kresky reached down and lifted her face by her chin until she was looking directly into his eyes. His expression had softened. She wasn't sure what she saw in his eyes. Pity? Compassion? His lips were now parted. His fingers moved softly to her cheek. Desire! How could she have missed that? She struggled to suppress a shudder.

"Perhaps we can work something out," he said.

The trembling had stopped. In place of her terror of immediate retribution was a gnawing dread, deep in her gut, about what the future held in store for her. This man was about to own her. He already owned her. He was just now asserting his claim.

Along with the immediacy of the scene in which she was immersed came memories of how she came to be there.

After Petra made her deal with Ethan and received her payment, she had no idea how to handle such a vast sum of money. It didn't take long for the vultures and scammers to find her. By the end of a year, she'd lost half her fortune. The biggest loss ironically was to a Ponzi scheme that claimed to be investing in making the Ambrosia Conversion available to the masses.

Desperate to recoup her losses, she'd turned to gambling. Not only did she lose the rest of her money, but she wound up deeply in debt, which is how Arlo Kresky wormed his way into her life. With a public face as a financier of technological ventures, he'd secretly generated much of his fortune as a loan shark with a ruthless underworld reputation. He'd found her in a casino soon after she'd lost the last few dollars of her fortune and began borrowing to cover her bets. Petra had been able to leverage his attraction to her to delay him from raining vengeance upon her for failing to repay. But her time was running out. It was time to pay one way or another.

"Perhaps we can work something out." His words hung in the air between them.

"What do you have in mind?"

The feelings Kresky had for her weren't mutual. He wasn't wholly repulsive, however, and was willing to forgive her entire debt if she married him. She'd also get to share his lavish lifestyle. This wouldn't be the first time she'd sold herself to get out of a tight spot.

Her body was now quiet. Her breathing had slowed again to a regular rhythm, to which she again found herself attending. The looming presence before her faded away and she was back in a world in which Arlo Kresky no longer existed. She felt, for just this moment, safe.

12

"**TAP, TAP, TAP.**" Connor announced his presence again via the kitchen door. "Tap, tap, tap."

She sprinted down the stairs to the kitchen and unlatched the door. Connor was inside in a flash and shut the door tightly behind him. He was breathing hard.

Before she could speak, his fingers were upon his lips to hush her. He spoke in a whisper.

"We have to leave, Petra. Right now." He began to catch his breath. "I think I've lost them for the moment, but they'll be here soon enough."

"Who?" she whispered. "Who's after us?"

"The cops. They've concluded that Arlo was murdered and we're both prime suspects."

"But if we're innocent…" She still had no idea whether either of them had been involved.

He shot her a look that made her think they weren t as innocent as she wanted to believe.

"We can't take any chances. We have to disappear. Grab what you need and let's go."

She had no idea what she'd need to take with her. Except for the few clothes that she'd worn in the days since the funeral, she had little idea what she owned, much less what she'd need to travel. She hadn't yet figured out how to access any of her or her husband's assets. She barely knew how to pay for groceries. And now she was going to have to sustain herself on the run. She looked to Connor for cues, but he'd taken off abruptly from his home and had arrived empty handed.

Suddenly, there was a pounding at the front door. Connor grabbed her by the hand and pulled her through the side door. They made their way quietly to the back of the house and disappeared through the rear gate to the street. They ducked behind a hedge just as the police car rounded a corner and watched it glide past them toward the bottom of the hill. After winding their way through back streets, they lucked into a taxi as they rounded a corner onto Beacon Street and jumped in.

The taxi lifted off the ground and headed for Boston. As they drove through Kenmore Square, she saw the blue lights closing in behind them. They had the driver stop abruptly at Boylston, jumped out and disappeared down an abandoned subway kiosk.

Trains and trolleys had stopped running in the underground maze of tunnels decades ago. For a few years, the stations became underground shopping malls, but even these were abandoned once shopping in the cloud had made brick and mortar commerce nearly obsolete. The city had boarded up the entrances to the underground system when it was abandoned, but adventurers had long since breached the barriers to pursue a modern urban variant of spelunking. At least with the third rails deenergized, the hazards of this sport were contained.

Once inside the station, they jumped off the platform and took off down a tunnel headed east toward Park Street. The sound of distant footsteps told them that their pursuers weren't far behind. At Park, the tunnels branched in all directions. The footsteps behind them were getting louder. They split up and agreed to meet at the vacuum tube station, which was their best hope of leaving the city.

Her breathing became labored as she sprinted down the southbound tunnel. The sound of Connor's steps receded behind her along with the steps of their pursuers. She heard the sharp ping of a laser gun firing, then silence. No more footsteps. Her heart sank, but she kept running until she reached the next station, ascended to the platform and emerged onto the street.

The entrance to the tube station was within sight. With her last burst of energy, she sprinted to the station and disappeared within it. The platform for the pod to DC was swarming with people. She wound her way through the crowd, managing to leverage the confusion to duck beneath the turnstile beam and boarded the pod. The doors closed. The pod began to accelerate just as she saw over her shoulder the first of the cops entering the station. Then she was hurtling at 4000 miles per hour toward her destination. Hopefully, her pursuers hadn't seen her board and would have no way to know which destination she'd chosen.

In just ten minutes, the pod began its deceleration, coming to a remarkably soft stop in the DC station. She disembarked and melted quickly into a rush hour crowd, hurrying home or to their chosen entertainment of the evening. The sides of skyscrapers were lit with images from the day's events. She stopped short in front of one such display that featured an image of Connor rising eight stories high. Other people were also watching this display and those who were standing on blue disks on the sidewalk seemed to be listening. She moved to a vacant blue disk. The narrator's voice came into focus as she adjusted her position.

"Connor Campbell was arrested today in Boston for the murder of financier Arlo Kresky and was taken to the Suffolk County detention facility. He has confessed to the crime and insists that he acted alone. But Petra Kresky, the victim's widow, remains a suspect. She eluded authorities this afternoon during the manhunt that resulted in Campbell's capture. Her current whereabouts are unknown."

She stared at the building as Connor's image dissolved and was replaced by an equally huge likeness of her. She tucked her head down, pulling her hair across her face, and hurried away from the image before anyone could recognize her.

So Connor had been caught. He'd sacrificed himself to save her when he drew their pursuers away. At least he'd survived the chase and whatever wounds he'd sustained. He was still alive, at least for now.

She was now a fugitive in another city she didn't know, alone and without resources. And she still had no idea who she was.

13

SHE SPENT THE NEXT several days going from homeless shelter to homeless shelter, hiding among the most forgotten souls in the city, begging for handouts to keep from starving. She spent much of her remaining time learning to explore the digital world by means of the artificial intelligence implant that integrated with her nervous system. While she lacked the vast capabilities of a MELD chip, which could access unlimited data within virtually any sphere of knowledge, her system enabled her to navigate her day to day world with considerable precision.

She pulled up the newsfeed for the day one morning while sitting in the rear of a coffee shop, having scored enough by panhandling to buy breakfast. Holographic images began to appear, coming into focus several feet in front of her. She was getting better at controlling her onboard digital processor and could now search for almost anything at will. Personal memories still remained the most elusive.

She sipped coffee as the images danced before her eyes and the news of the day unfolded in the periphery of her awareness. Then a figure appeared that commanded her attention. She put down her coffee and stared. A regal looking man, well over six feet tall, with sculpted features crowned with a gleaming bald head and robed in royal blue silk, was about to speak. Something about his bearing tugged at a memory buried deep within her. His name was on the tip of her tongue. When he began to speak, his voice reached for the buried memory, its resonance seeming to encircle it, tugging, seeking.

Someone introduced him as Marcus Takana, Minister of Discovery. He was a prominent public figure. Of course she would recognize him. Nothing personal. Just someone in the public eye. And yet...there was something more. She could almost feel the tug.

"We are on the brink of breakthroughs," Takana began, "that will elevate the lives of all sentient beings, whether carbon or silicon based."

The scene shifted to show the audience reaction. Some of the people were on their feet cheering, while others held placards aloft decrying those who would grant SPUDs the same rights as flesh and blood humans.

As the camera panned the crowd and zoomed in, something else captured her attention. She froze the frame and zoomed in closer on a slender, Asian-looking man. Looking even closer, she saw blue eyes that shone brightly, framed by brown skin. Ethan! What was he doing at Minister Takana's speech? There had to be a connection.

Exploring the archives of the UDB for stories about Marcus Takana, she discovered a recent attempt on his life that had occurred during a speech in San Francisco. The date of this event stunned her. It was the same day as Arlo Kresky's funeral, the day she emerged into consciousness in Petra Kresky's body in the middle of the afternoon.

The attack, which had commenced at the stroke of noon, had been the work of the Tribe of 23, an anti-SPUD hate group, and had been foiled by a mystery woman who'd died at the scene. Two other people died that day: Hector Lasko, one of the would-be assassins, and Raymond Mettler, the reclusive billionaire who'd created HibernaTurf. Why would Mettler have been at Takana's speech?

One other remarkable detail caught her attention. When the authorities came to clean up the carnage at the hotel where the talk took place, the woman's body had vanished. Nobody saw what happened to it. Even in the recordings of the scene of the attack, the body was there one moment and gone the next. Like magic. Attempts to identify her face came up empty. She was like a ghost on the UDB. The one detail of her appearance upon which every eye witness agreed was her flaming red hair.

"Raymond Mettler," she thought. "I know that name, too, and not just because he was famous. He's also a part of this mystery."

There were just too many coincidences to ignore. Could the mystery woman be the other half of Petra's contract with Ethan? And if so, who was she and what was she doing at Marcus Takana's talk the day she died saving his life?

She searched for the holographic record of that day. It began with footage of the moderator introducing the Artificial Cognition Conference, followed by a talk by an expert in longevity research. Then Marcus Takana was introduced and strode to the podium amidst thunderous applause. He began to speak, and suddenly the images dissolved, purged from the UDB as mysteriously as the redhead's body had disappeared from the scene of the crime.

She retrieved the record again, starting it at the beginning of Takana's speech. This time, something about the cadence of his speech, compared with his more recent speech, seemed off. Almost like it wasn't the same person. She went back again to the beginning to listen more closely, and now another detail: the sound of a bell tower in the background sounding the hour.

Suddenly, the pain stabbed at the base of her skull, more intensely than ever before. The coffee shop disappeared, and she was in a massive ballroom, standing at the rear. Marcus Takana was on the stage way in front of where she stood across a sea of heads. She was scanning the room, looking for something or someone. As she swung her head around, long red hair whirled before her eyes.

Then she was standing on a balcony, grappling with a powerful giant with rugged features and wavy blond hair. She, too, was strong, holding her own in the struggle. She could see the bell tower over the railing as the bells pealed. She felt herself lunge for his feet, grab him by the ankles, and hurl him over the railing, then heard the lethal thud as he hit the ground.

"Terra!" she heard clearly over her shoulder. Then the pain was there again at the base of her skull, excruciating, explosive. And everything went black.

She was back in the present, watching the holographic Takana speak. Memories started streaming back.

A child of ten sitting by the bedside of a frail and pallid woman. "Don't die, Mama." Her own voice. "Please don't die. I need you." The woman's palm sliding over her little hand.

"Don't worry, Theresa." Her mother's voice. "You're strong. You'll survive and live a long, long time. You'll see."

An adult, covered head to toe in a burka, standing in a desert in front of a low stone building with a barred window in the door, lighting a fuse...the door blowing open.

"Terra." Macklyn's voice. "I knew you'd come back for me."

Macklyn again. Lying in each other's arms, Macklyn whispering her name in her ear: "Terra," the softness of the whispered word expressing the tenderness of this powerhouse of a woman capable of killing with her bare hands.

Standing in front of a man sitting backlit, his face in shadows, gnarled hands folded on the desk in front of him.

"Terra." The Director's voice. "We've been watching you. You've been selected for an extraordinary mission. We hope you'll agree that it will be worth leaving everything and everyone else in your life until now behind. Your country needs you."

"Terra," she thought. "That's me. That's who I am...or was. She died on that balcony and came back in Petra's body. The contract Petra made with Ethan...I was the other half."

14

WITH THE REVELATION of her name, the door to Terra's past burst open like the door to the Saudi prison from which she'd helped Macklyn escape.

Terra had worked as an agent for Ganymede, the same organization that employed Ethan, as a broker of contracts between wealthy older clients and healthy younger individuals on the margins of society that would enable the old when they died to inhabit the bodies of their younger counterparts. Raymond Mettler and Marcus Takana had been one such pair.

Because her job entailed substantial risk, Terra had been granted a contract by her employer so that she could continue her work should she meet with an untimely death. But the massive brain trauma that had accompanied her death had scrambled her memories when her consciousness jumped to Petra's body. Now that the details of her past were again accessible, she wondered whether there might still be other aspects of her identity that were immutably changed. For one thing, she wasn't sure that returning to her work with Ganymede was how she wanted to spend her second life.

In her former life, Terra had gained secure access using biometric data intrinsic to the body she no longer possessed. If she were to get into Ganymede or even her own home and finances, she would need a way past this security. She'd made provisions years ago for the possibility that she'd need such access while dwelling in another body. Now was the time to harvest the fruits of her foresight.

She found the tablet computer in an out of the way antique shop, run by an aging hacker with an affinity for ancient hardware. Originally manufactured in the mid-twenties, it was one of the last such devices made before wearable hardware made freestanding computers obsolete. It wasn't long before most interfaces became implantable and fully integrated with the senses. MELD chips came later, seamlessly integrating all the information on the Universal Data Base with native intelligence. While increasingly common in the last decade, these remained relatively expensive and still available mostly to the privileged. Terra had enjoyed the luxury of a MELD chip, but Petra had not deemed it a priority, leaving Terra to navigate her new digital world with more limited resources.

For some purposes, however, ancient hardware carried certain advantages. Personal privacy had largely been sacrificed with the integration of hardware with the body. The governments of the world had long ago forbidden anonymous access to the UDB. But a freestanding computer could be used as a "burner" without identifying the user and jettisoned once its purpose was accomplished. Tablets could also still access the Dark Web using Tor, a browser developed in the 1990's by the United States government, enabling access to the UDB while making the origin of the search untraceable. Terra had used just such a tablet with the Tor browser to save the encrypted files she was now about to retrieve.

She sat on a park bench with the tablet on her lap. Sometimes clandestine activity is best accomplished in plain sight. In the event that her digital activity did get traced to her location, she would be long gone by the time anyone got there. She placed her finger over the heat sensitive port on the edge of the tablet and held it a few seconds. It came to life. She breathed a sigh of relief. The generation of batteries that powered these last computers was particularly robust.

She looked for the Tor browser on the tablet, but it was nowhere to be seen. If she tried to download it from the UDB, her activity could be detected and traced, defeating the purpose of using it. The several megabytes of code required to create the browser from scratch exceeded the capacity of even her prodigious memory and would have taken far too long to transcribe even if she knew it. She would have to work fast enough to compensate for traceability.

It took only moments to find the digital lockbox where she'd stored her most private files. It was secured old school with a random string of 24 characters that she'd committed to memory. She typed them in, and the list of files appeared. She scrolled down to a file entitled "me.clone" and opened it. The contents were intact. She found the tiny port on the edge of the tablet and inserted a needle sized cylinder much like the one that Ethan had passed her containing Petra's memories. She downloaded the file to the memory module, removed it, and slipped it into a tiny opening on the rim of her shoe. Then she erased the tablet, tossed it in the river, and watched it float downstream.

Her next quest would be more difficult. She'd need to secure the hardware needed to execute the programs she'd just recovered, a bioprinter capable of both mimicking human tissue and implanting it with a DNA signature. These were now mostly used in hospitals. She located a small community hospital that would have minimal security, entered through the emergency entrance and slipped past the receiving area to the laboratories. No bioprinting had been scheduled that night. The laboratory was dark. It was child's play for a former clandestine operative to break in.

She found the printer, turned it on, and slipped the memory module into an available port. She scrolled down the files that came up on the screen and clicked one called "eyes." The machine came to life. Within ten minutes, a pair of microthin contact lenses had been generated. They were emerald green in color, exactly the native color of her eyes.

They also contained a retinal pattern embedded in the center over the iris that would read exactly like her native retinas.

She scrolled down further to select a file that said "hands." The machine printed out ten identical pairs of hand shaped film. These would be applied to her palms to duplicate not only her palm prints, but also her DNA. Once applied, they would bond tightly to her own tissues until the cells naturally shed like native skin. Each pair might last up to a week.

Lastly, she selected a file called "hair." The machine deposited a dozen droplets of a clear gel, each sealed within a glass bubble. Once inoculated onto her scalp, their DNA code would change her hair to her native color and texture. Not only did she anticipate future situations in which it would be convenient to resemble her former self, but she also saw an advantage to completing a disguise that could make Petra vanish from the radar of those who pursued her.

She ejected the module, turned off the printer, and sipped unnoticed from the lab, her package of precious tissues tucked snugly against the skin below her navel. It had been a productive day's work. Neither her memory nor her skills had failed her.

Terra's next destination was Georgetown where she'd lived for most of her tenure with Ganymede. One of the perks of working as an operative for a clandestine government unit was sufficient wealth to enjoy substantial luxury. She made her way to 33rd Street NW and found the entrance to a red brick building that overlooked the Potomac. The ground floor and basement had flooded in the thirties when the river overflowed its banks inundating much of the city, but the levees built toward the end of that decade had held and the property had been fully restored.

Before entering the building, she applied a set of hand film to her hands and put on the contact lenses. Once inside, she found the elevators and summoned the one that would go all the way to the penthouse level. The elevator doors opened.

She stepped inside the glass cylinder, placed her index finger on the small pad beside the indicator for the penthouse, and waited. A brief whirring sound signified that the reader had sampled the DNA on her fingertip. The doors closed. The cylinder sealed itself and shot all the way to the top floor, coming to a remarkably soft stop at its destination. The cylinder opened. She was home.

Terra scanned the entry to the penthouse for signs of intruders during her absence. She moved methodically from room to room, inspecting each space minutely. She had anticipated that Ganymede might have raided the apartment after her death and liquidated it, but there was no sign that anyone else had been there. Perhaps the apartment was an oversight. Perhaps they left it intact, expecting that she might return to it in her new body and they were planning for her to resume work as their operative once she'd accommodated to her new circumstances. Or perhaps it was left as a trap that would enable them to track her until her loyalty could be determined.

It felt wonderful to be back on familiar ground, even if still within a stranger's body. She couldn't wait to get out of Petra's clothes and into her own outer skin, but paused briefly to gaze out over the balcony at the Potomac, a view that always managed to soothe her regardless of the intensity of her day.

She headed to the bathroom, stripped off her clothing and stepped into the transparent cleansing pod. A vertical row of three touchpads was on the wall to her right. She touched the top pad and jets all around her shot a mist that coated her from head to toe. She touched the middle pad and blasts of air blew her dry. She touched the third and more jets covered her body with a viscous liquid that left her skin feeling like silk. She passed both hands down the front of her body and luxuriated in the slickness.

Next she headed to the wardrobe. In the middle of the room stood another pod, similar in size to the cleansing pod, but opaque. In her previous life, she'd preferred the freedom of spray-on clothing for covert missions. It suited her body with its slender profile, tight skin, and complete absence of body hair. It enabled her movements to be unencumbered, an advantage in situations that required nimble movements and in physical confrontations in which the advantage might turn on a dime. The slickness of her skin was preserved, which improved her chance of avoiding an adversary's grasp.

The printing pod had been programmed with patterns matched precisely to the contours of her body. While Petra's form was similar enough for Terra's clothes to fit well, the paint patterns were less forgiving. When time permitted, she'd scan her body and generate a new set of patterns.

Terra sorted through the form fitting outfits that she'd worn for work in situations where the spray clothing provided inadequate protection, then through the looser garments she'd worn for play, ranging from opaque to diaphanous. She held the edge of one particularly sensuous number between a thumb and forefinger to sample the texture. It had been one of Macklyn's favorites.

Her thoughts drifted back to the last time she and Macklyn had been together. It was long ago, just after she was drafted into service with Ganymede. She'd been forbidden to continue any of her relationships with her colleagues at the NSA, but had managed to slip away for one last rendezvous with Macklyn before dropping out of sight. She couldn't tell Macklyn why they could never see each other again. She couldn't even say goodbye because there would be too many questions that she couldn't answer, and she could never trust herself to keep secrets from Macklyn. The passion she brought to their bed that night, though, must have told Macklyn that something extraordinary was about to happen. She'd fervently hoped that Macklyn had forgiven her for disappearing.

New questions began to surface, first as indistinct whispers, then later as compelling dilemmas. When she died, what became of her promises to Ganymede? Did they still own her in her new life or did dying mean a fresh start? And was she now free to reconnect with Macklyn...if she could find her...if she were still available or even still alive?

And what about Connor? Now that she'd had a taste of love with a man in this strange new home of a body, was Macklyn still what she'd want? Would this body respond to a woman's touch as hers had to Macklyn's or was she now fundamentally changed in ways that she could never undo?

15

SHE APPROACHED the door to the flat that had been her and Macklyn's love nest almost twenty years ago. She was relieved to see that the building still existed, but it was a very long shot that Macklyn had maintained the apartment all these years and even more unlikely that she'd not removed Terra's identity from its security. She held her breath as she placed her forefinger on the pad.

There was a long silence, followed by a faint whirring, then a click. She gently pushed the door and it gave way, opening about a foot before creaking to a stop. It was dark inside. She listened at the opening. No sounds. No movements. She pushed again and the door opened wider. She tiptoed barefoot across the threshold into the space.

The faint sound of breathing came from behind her. She ducked in time to deflect a blow to her head, grabbed her assailant by the arm, thrust out her leg, and pulled. The body hit the ground with a sharp thud and Terra pinned it to the floor with hers. An arm shot up to her left and a ray of light reflected off her eye and caught the glint of a knife blade coming at her, suddenly stopping short of its mark. A gasp.

"Terra?" The voice was Macklyn's, bewildered, tentative.

Terra's eyes were now adjusting to the darkness. Macklyn's face took form, emerging from the shadows. Years older than she remembered her, but unmistakably Macklyn.

"Macklyn," Terra answered. "It's me."

"But how?" Macklyn asked. "I heard you'd been killed."

"I was...but I'm back. It's a very long story."

Macklyn's eyes also began adjusting to the light. Terra's telltale emerald eyes had stayed her hand in the fight, but as the rest of her features took form, Macklyn's eyes widened with renewed alarm.

"Who are you?" Macklyn cried out, her body stiffening. "You look like a stranger." She reached again for the knife that was now lying on the floor beside them. Terra's hand shot out and grabbed her by the wrist.

"Macklyn, it's me," Terra repeated. "Not exactly my body, but still me." She lowered her face to Macklyn's, ran her tongue around Macklyn's open lips, then pressed their lips softly, tenderly together. Macklyn responded with her own tongue. Her body relaxed and her arms enfolded Terra in a hungry embrace.

Macklyn's passion ruled the moment. Terra followed willingly, even joyfully. Nothing in her life had ever brought the comfort of Macklyn's embrace. Never had she felt safer than in Macklyn's presence. But the passion that began with the kiss subsided, then felt forced. And there were moments while they made love that she imagined Connor astride her in Macklyn's place.

"Who am I?" Terra wondered. "Who have I become? Can I still be me in this other body or am I turning into her, into Petra? Has a part of her been left behind to reclaim her body...or to make me share it?"

Terra slept that night in Macklyn's arms, feeling safe for the first time since she'd awakened in her new skin, safer perhaps than she'd felt ever since Ganymede poached her from the NSA and banished Macklyn from her life. Even without the passion that had fueled their love so many years ago, her love still burned brightly and her trust was deep for this woman who always had her back.

No more words passed between them that night, no explanation of the bizarre circumstances of Terra's metamorphosis. Macklyn, for her part, raised no further questions about Terra's identity. The last thing that Terra felt that night before falling into peaceful slumber was a gentle, loving squeeze that welcomed her home.

Terra awoke the next morning to the smell of coffee. Not just any coffee, but the exquisite aroma of the blend from the Rwandan Rift Valley for which they'd shared a special fondness when they were together. As she sipped across the table from Macklyn, the years were momentarily erased and she imagined Macklyn's face as it had been when they'd last parted, slender and flawless, without the crow's feet in the corners of her eyes or the fine lines that radiated from the corners of her mouth. When her present-day features came back into focus, Terra was drawn into the softness of her smile and the ebony depths of her eyes.

"You must have a lot of questions," Terra said between sips.

"They can wait until you're ready to tell me."

"Did you ever wonder what happened to me when I disappeared?"

"Of course I did. I looked high and low for you, but even with my resources at the agency, I always came up empty. I thought perhaps you'd been captured or died. On the grid, it was as though you'd never existed. You became a ghost."

Terra put down her cup, looked away and considered how much she could tell Macklyn, even now. When she again looked forward to make eye contact, she'd decided that there was no reason to hold anything back.

"Have you ever heard of Ganymede?" Terra asked.

"I'd heard rumors long ago within the agency's grapevine of an ultra deep cover operation created to replace foreign despots with imposters. It had supposedly been conceived as a desperate response to a North Korean dictator who got dangerously close to being able to destroy the world. When he was assassinated and a revolution replaced his regime with a moderate leader, Ganymede receded into the obscure mythology of abolished projects."

"What if I told you that Ganymede was real and still very much alive?"

"It would be hard to believe that such a project could go on for decades under the radar of the NSA. Why would it even still exist?"

"I've wondered about that myself. But I can assure you that it does. When I disappeared it was within Ganymede's shroud of secrecy, and I had little choice but to do their bidding without questioning their agenda."

"So what was it that they had you do?"

"They'd developed technology that permitted the transfer of consciousness between bodies. They were applying it for profit by selling wealthy older people the opportunity to occupy a young person's body when they died. They contracted with young people in pristine health to surrender the rights to their bodies for a portion of the bounties they collected. Their methods were advanced. Proving and refining them was another agenda for creating these contracts."

"And your role…?" asked Macklyn.

"Was as broker for the contracts." Terra replied. "I met separately with the buyers and sellers to negotiate their roles. I was also responsible for keeping these transactions anonymous."

"It sounds creepy."

"It was. My job required me to be ruthless, but as time went on, I had lots of misgivings. Some of the people who lost their lives were decent. It got to where I hated to see any of them die. But there wasn't anything I could do to stop it except try to prolong the lives of the buyers. Usually it was out of my hands. I was trying to save one such pair when I was killed."

"Killed?"

"Yes, shot through the back of the head. I died instantly."

"Then how…?"

"My job was dangerous. I'd been given the Ambrosia Conversion to stop me from aging and protect me from natural infirmity and death, but my superiors foresaw that I might still be killed. They provided me a contract as insurance against my dying. This is the body I got when mine died. It belonged to a woman named Petra Kresky."

"And what happened to her?"

"She died in my body when my mind jumped to hers. She no longer exists." Terra wasn't sure, however, that this was entirely true. Aspects of Petra seemed to be lingering within her. And her memories still resided on the memory stick that Terra carried within the port in her thigh. There was more to learn about the woman whose body she now possessed.

Terra told Macklyn about her awakening within Petra's body, her amnesia, and her journey back to awareness of who she was.

"Amnesia was never an anticipated side effect of the mind transfers," Terra explained. "I figure that the massive trauma my brain sustained at the moment of death scrambled the data that was drawn from it so that my memories accompanied my consciousness in an encrypted form."

She described her struggle to learn enough about Petra Kresky to become her and her eventual flight when Petra became a suspect in her husband's death. She shared that Petra seemed to have had a lover, but left out that she, Terra, had continued that relationship and had fallen in love with him, too. And she did not tell Macklyn how in Petra's body lustful thoughts had taken an entirely unexpected turn.

16

TERRA AWOKE with the first rays of sun filtering through the east window of their bedroom, an unfamiliar sensation rising in the back of her throat.

"Nausea," she thought. Since she'd had the Ambrosia Conversion, she'd been in near perfect health. And since Petra's body had also had the Conversion, she'd continued to be free of the day to day symptoms that many people still experienced even in the middle of the twenty-first century.

She thought back to what she'd eaten the night before. Nothing unusual. She got out of bed quietly, leaving Macklyn still slumbering, stripped off her clothes, and stood before the full-length bathroom mirror. Perhaps it was her imagination, but her nipples appeared redder than usual. She ran her hands down over her breasts and across her nipples. They were tender to her touch, another unaccustomed sensation.

"No. Can't be," she thought.

She sat on the toilet and caught the first flow of urine in a jar. There was once a time when women had to buy pregnancy tests at a pharmacy. Now they were a routine part of the digital battery of medical tests in every home. But a few drops of urine were still required.

Terra scanned the sample with the wand. Positive. Now what?

Pregnancy was never something she'd had to worry about in her previous life, given her sexual orientation. And it was never something she'd considered choosing. It would have been anathema to her work as a covert operative to sustain a pregnancy and raise a child.

She thought back over the weeks since she'd assumed Petra Kresky's identity. She'd last been intimate with Connor nearly three weeks before, just prior to their flight and his arrest. The timing seemed right. But little enough time had passed since the exchange that conception could have occurred on Petra's watch. And if that were the case, was the baby Connor's or Arlo Kresky's?

Yet another wrinkle occurred to Terra. This child would carry Petra's genes, not hers. If she carried it to term, whose child would it be? Would she be just a surrogate bringing Petra's child into the world to continue her legacy or would the child be hers? Because after all, she and Petra were now biologically identical.

A more immediate dilemma was Macklyn. She'd be hard pressed to hide her physical changes from the trained eye of another spy. And so far, she'd not shared with Macklyn her recent adventures in her heterosexual world. How would Macklyn take it? If Terra wanted Macklyn as a partner in raising a child, would she be willing?

She dressed and made coffee before waking Macklyn. She'd had time to compose herself. There would be no need for confrontation, at least not this morning.

It took just a few days for the morning sickness to resolve. It was replaced with feelings equally unfamiliar, but far more pleasant. She felt a heightened sense of sensuality, with especially sharpened smell and touch. And it took little to arouse her sexually. Even within Petra's body, she found herself craving physical contact with Macklyn and was almost as responsive to her touch as she'd been in her own skin. While she still fantasized about Connor, she felt at home again in Macklyn's bed.

As the days passed, the thought of leaving Macklyn behind again for Ganymede became less and less tenable. The power of the Director's grasp upon her was diminishing. Blind loyalty was giving way to a clearer, more nuanced view of the mission to which she'd devoted nearly two decades of her life. The zeal of her fellow operatives had infected her and clouded her judgment. Not the least of these had been Ethan, who'd been her handler during her training before she'd earned the Director's trust to work independently. Now that she'd had a taste of Ethan's methods through Petra's eyes, she wondered how she could ever have looked up to him. And she shuddered to think that she'd become as cold-blooded as he was.

She doubted that she'd seen the last of Ethan. He knew she'd made the jump to Petra's body and had already made contact with her as Petra. While her physical transition back to Terra might fool the authorities who were searching for Petra, it would provide no cover from Ethan or from Ganymede. And there was still the loose end of Ethan's presence at Marcus Takana's speech. Had he been hoping that Terra would also show up in the crowd? It was only a matter of time before she'd have to face him. And she couldn't imagine a more formidable adversary.

17

AS TERRA SIPPED her morning coffee nearly two weeks after discovering she was pregnant, she performed her daily UDB search for news of Connor. Nothing had turned up for more than a month. But today her persistence was rewarded.

"ACCUSED MURDERER ESCAPES" blared the headline. She hungrily absorbed the data that followed. Connor had vanished during the night in the midst of a total shutdown of the prison's security network. Given the sophistication and redundancy within the system, the authorities speculated that it had been disabled by highly skilled hackers. The shutdown had been brief and his extraction swift. No other prisoners had escaped, so it seemed evident that his escape was the sole purpose of the hack. While the prisoner had been implanted with a tracking device, it had been disabled. His whereabouts were unknown.

Terra felt a thrill from the possibility of seeing Connor again, although she had no idea how they might find each other. She hid her excitement from Macklyn as best she could. When Terra ventured a glance in her direction, however, Macklyn's expression made it obvious that she knew something was up. Terra rose from the table and started to leave the room.

"Something of interest in the news?" Macklyn asked before she could complete her retreat. Terra considered how much she could say and settled on a partial truth.

"Yeah," she replied, turning to face Macklyn after a too long pause. "The man who was accused of murdering Petra's husband has escaped from prison." Macklyn's expression changed as she scrutinized Terra's face. The furrows in her forehead deepened over narrowed eyes.

"So what does that mean to you," Macklyn asked. "Is that a good thing or a bad thing?"

'Hard to know," Terra replied, now lying outright. "If he killed Petra's husband, he might come after me."

Macklyn wasn't buying it. Terra had been unable to conceal her excitement or to pass it off as fear.

"Be careful, Terra," Macklyn warned. "Whatever you think you know about him you need to take with a grain of salt. Everyone in Petra's life before you got there is a stranger to you."

Connor was indeed a stranger, a stranger with apparently very powerful friends who were willing to take big risks to spring him from prison. What was a journalist doing with such friends? And why had he really infiltrated Kresky's life, and Petra's? Perhaps he indeed meant her harm and would come after her to complete whatever mission he'd been sent to accomplish.

"I'll watch my back," Terra acknowledged. "Point taken."

As Terra drew near the end of her early morning run in the park the next day, she suddenly felt the hairs bristle on the back of her neck and guessed she was being watched. She quickened her pace, attending closely to her surroundings. She was still blindsided at a sharp turn on the path when an arm encircled her from behind and a hand covered her mouth.

"Petra, shhh!" came a whispered command. "It's me...Connor."

Her heart filled at the same time with apprehension and joy. He'd been all she could think about these many weeks and now he was here. But so many things about his presence were red flags. How had he found her, a needle in a haystack who'd managed to hide from a nationwide manhunt?

When they'd last parted, she was still Petra as far as he knew. But she'd drastically changed her appearance to become Terra again. Her hair had by now changed all the way back to the flaming red that had been Terra's most striking feature along with her emerald eyes. It had grown out enough that when Terra caught sight of herself in the mirror from a distance, she looked a lot like her old self. And yet Connor knew her as Petra despite the disguise.

Connor released the pressure of the hand over her mouth and slowly drew it away. She remained silent as she turned to look at him. He, too, was in disguise, now wearing a full beard and mustache. But she knew him by his eyes and by his lips. She drew away when he tried to kiss her.

"How did you find me, Connor?" she demanded. "And who the hell are you really?"

"What do you mean?"

"You have powerful friends who could break you out of prison and help you find me. They didn't come out of the blue. There seems to be a lot you haven't told me."

"You're right, Petra," Connor said. "I'm not who you thought I was. I'll tell you everything when the time is right, but first we must get to safety."

"What does that even mean? I felt safe enough here until you showed up. Now I'm not so sure. I have no idea who I can trust."

"The way I found you, others can find you, too. You're far safer with me than with the alternatives. And we both need to disappear soon while we still have the chance."

As he spoke, her face flushed and her right forefinger went to the tiny bump behind her ear. How could she have forgotten that it was a way to track her? She'd watched similar devices implanted in her former clients and had been familiar with all its capabilities. She'd used them to track her clients when she worked for Ganymede and should have removed it the moment her memory returned.

She desperately wanted to trust Connor, even with all her alarms sounding. He was the one thing that gave meaning to her life as Petra, just as Macklyn had given meaning to Terra's life. Could there now be room in her life for them both?

"I'm not who you thought I was either," Terra said.

"I know," Connor replied, putting a finger on her lips. "I know who you are. That's why I'm here."

18

WHEN TERRA got back to the apartment after her encounter with Connor, she was relieved to find Macklyn gone. She'd have some distance from the meeting and time to compose herself before facing Macklyn's scrutiny. Her first order of business was to extract the transducer from behind her ear.

Terra found the surgical first aid kit that they'd always kept for emergencies. It contained, among other things, a small scalpel with a triangular blade that came to a sharp point. She pulled the skin on her neck tight just below the pea sized bump and inserted the blade at the lower edge of the nodule. With a swift motion, she encircled it with a clean incision that undercut the transducer, then popped it out with her forefinger. Blood oozed around the incision. She covered it with a small bandage, confident from prior experience that the wound would heal rapidly and cleanly. She tossed the tiny device into a coffee grinder and reduced it to a pile of sand.

Terra had no illusions that the transducer hadn't already been used to track her by more than just Connor's associates. Her suspicions were confirmed the next morning when she looked out the window to see a bright red two-seater parked on the street. The car bore no markings, but its sleek lines and sapphire colored windshield were one of a kind.

"My car," Terra thought. She pondered the wisdom of approaching it, but her curiosity won. There were still so many questions that needed answers, even if it meant taking risks.

As she walked up to the driver's door, it opened to meet her. She looked inside. It was empty. She sat in the driver's seat and placed her fingertip on the biometric sensor on the dashboard. The instruments lit up. The door closed and the car lifted off the ground. She discovered quickly that the steering was disabled. The car was driving itself to a preprogrammed destination. She sat back and surrendered to the ride.

The last few turns brought her into familiar territory. When the car veered from the road into a steep tunnel, she recognized the approach to Ganymede's Washington DC station. Once inside the underground chamber, the car settled to a stop. The doors opened. A hand reached in to help her out.

She looked up to see the dark-skinned young man with the piercing blue eyes who had bumped her on the street and passed her the module that contained Petra's memories.

"Hello, Ethan," she said. "It's been a long time."

"Hello, Terra," Ethan said. "Good to see you again. Sorry about your accident."

"A little more than an accident." She smiled wryly. "So why am I here?"

"Come with me." He led her to a door on the far side of the chamber and knocked.

"Come in," came a raspy voice from the other side of the door. "It's open."

Once inside, Terra found herself face to face with a man she'd seen only once before, at the time that she was first recruited by Ganymede. Like before, he was backlit, leaving his face in shadows. He remained nameless.

"Welcome back, Terra," said the faceless man. "You've had a long journey." He folded his hands on the desk in front of him. Veins and tendons showed through wrinkled, paper thin skin. The knuckles of the distal joints were gnarled, bending the tips of the index and middle fingers of both hands slightly outward from the thumbs. She was certain that she could pick out the Director in any crowd by his hands.

"What am I doing here?" she asked.

"You don't think we went to all this trouble just to have you walk off into the sunset, do you?" he replied. "You've been much too valuable an asset. It would be a terrible shame for your skills to go to waste."

"But I'm not exactly myself, as you can see," she said, sweeping her hand down the length of her body. "And I come with baggage from someone else's life."

"You've already done an impressive job of recreating your identity. We can help wipe away some of the remaining traces of Petra Kresky. As you know, our technology is advanced. It's also quite versatile."

Terra wondered how far Ganymede had progressed in duplicating identity. She had little doubt that they could make her look more like herself. But what about some of the other essential qualities that differentiated Terra from Petra? What, for example, would become of her sexuality, and of her feelings for Connor?

"I expect you've been very confused," said the man, as if reading her mind. "You've inherited relationships from your benefactor, relationships that could pose considerable danger."

"What do you mean?"

"We have reason to believe that the man who was arrested for killing Petra's husband is an agent planted in her house by Mandala to sabotage our project."

"What's Mandala?"

"A group sworn to expose us and to bring us down, subversives who oppose the very idea of immortality, who believe that death is a necessary part of life. Do you remember when hackers took over the minds of several of our pairs of subjects? They ran virtual scenarios that simulated the deaths of the buyers, triggering the exchanges. The scripts were so convincing that several of them wound up actually dying. Others narrowly escaped."

"That was Mandala?"

"It was. And hacking is just one of the tactics they've been using. They've also planted agents in the lives of some of our subjects, including Petra Kresky. Things got messy for that agent when he fell in love with his target and messier still when her husband was killed."

So they knew about Connor's involvement with her. If what she was hearing was true, they knew far more about him than she did.

"We're trusting you to lose him," the Director went on, "with extreme prejudice if that's what it takes. Perhaps you can just make sure that the authorities find him and take him back into custody. Meanwhile, we plan to reassign you when the time is right. You can keep your car. We understand you were very attached to it. And we'll return it to your control."

"Then what happens?"

"Once you've taken care of this Connor matter, we'll be in touch. Ethan will be your contact. He'll find you, even without the transducer you've so conveniently destroyed. One last thing," he continued, handing her a vial. "Put three drops of this under your tongue every night before you sleep. It will turn your skin white within a week. You'll look almost like your old self."

She took the vial and returned to the space where she'd left the car. The doors opened to her approach. She got in, started the motor, and ascended the tunnel into daylight.

Terra couldn't be sure whether or not Connor was the enemy, but the evidence looked grim. And now she was charged with destroying him one way or another.

And what, she wondered, of Macklyn? If Ganymede had been tracking Terra and knew about Connor, then surely they knew about Macklyn as well. But there was no mention of her in this meeting. Did they know that she'd told Macklyn about them? Would they eventually insist on eliminating her, too? She felt as if the whole weight of the world was on her shoulders. And she could turn to neither of the people she'd trusted until then to share that weight.

19

WHEN TERRA AND CONNOR last parted, he'd shared nothing about where to find him. He told her that he'd find her when the time was right to meet again. Given what she'd learned at Ganymede, his secretiveness left her less and less inclined to trust him. She figured he already knew where she was staying, so hiding from him at this point would mean leaving Macklyn again, which she was unwilling to do. All she could do now was wait until he showed up.

Five days passed. She ran daily in the park at the same time each morning, expecting him to turn up any time. At the end of her run on the sixth day, she sensed that she was being watched, turned suddenly down a side path, and doubled back through the trees. Connor was still looking for her when she took him from behind, pulled him into the trees, and placed the edge of a knife against his throat.

"Tell me why I shouldn't just kill you now," she hissed, drawing the blade closer.

"Because I've saved you once already when I sacrificed myself in the tunnels to let you escape," Connor replied. "Because you know I'd never do anything to hurt you."

"I don't know that," Terra said. "All I know is that you've lied to me from the beginning."

"And I don't want to lie anymore. I'm ready to tell you everything. Then you can judge whether or not I should die. But it would be easier to talk without a knife at my throat."

As angry as she was, she felt a thrill from the contact between their bodies and couldn't shake the desire deep within her to be with him again. She desperately wanted to believe him...to erase the chasm of mistrust that was keeping them apart. And she had no idea whether or not she had the fortitude to kill him even if he deserved to die.

She drew the blade away from his neck and gave him a shove with her knee, still holding the knife. He turned to face her.

"Sit down," she commanded. Connor sat on the ground. She sat opposite him, knife in hand.

"I wouldn't bet your life on outrunning me," she said. "You'll get up when I tell you to get up. Now start talking."

"Terra," he began. "I guess I should call you Terra now because that's who you really are. I was recruited by an organization called Mandala to get close to Petra Kresky." He paused and breathed deeply.

So far, at least, what he was telling her fit with the information from Ganymede.

"I was to gain her trust," he continued. "I was told that she was part of an experiment by a secret government agency to exchange consciousness between bodies and confer virtual immortality upon a privileged few at the expense of less fortunate others. Petra was one of the prospective victims and I eventually learned that you were the beneficiary of her sacrifice."

Terra felt a twinge of remorse as she listened, realizing that an innocent person had died in her place, however willingly she'd entered into the contract.

"Mandala's mission was to stop the experiment at all cost."

"Were you supposed to kill her?" Terra asked.

"Quite the contrary. I was supposed to gain her trust, then convince her to renege on the contract and remove the transducer. I was getting close to showing my hand when the exchange occurred."

"So you knew?"

"Not right away. But I heard about the attempt on Takana's life and the redhead killed at the scene and put two and two together. I contacted Mandala and they confirmed my suspicion."

"So who were you making love to? Her or me?" Terra demanded. "Or were you just pretending in order not to blow your cover."

"It's complicated, Terra, believe me. I didn't plan to fall in love with her, but I did in spite of myself. And when Kresky died, I imagined that we could be together."

"Did you kill him?"

"No. I was as surprised as anyone when he died."

"Did she? Because if she did, I haven't recovered that part of her memory yet."

"I really don't know. She'd talked about wanting him to die, but never said she was planning to do it. And you became her before I could ask her."

"So what about us?" Terra pressed.

"When we met for the first time after the exchange, I thought you were still her. By the time I realized that you weren't, we'd already connected. She was the bridge between us. It was easy to fall in love with you."

"With me...you mean with my body. It was just a physical connection."

"At first, yes. But like I said, it's complicated. It feels like there's still a small part of her there inside you. But being with you was exciting. Petra was endearing, but guileless. You were mysterious and resourceful. The way you handled your amnesia and learned to navigate your new world was brilliant. I could tell I was with someone extraordinary."

"So did you come back for me or are you still working for Mandala?"

"Both," Connor said. "I had to see you again, to be with you again, but…" He searched for words. "Mandala still has an agenda that involves us both."

"An agenda…"

"To stop the experiments. To stop Ganymede. You must have figured out by now how crazy it all is...how evil. It goes even beyond having people die in place of others. That was enough for Mandala to set out to stop them. But we have reason to believe they plan to use it to control governments...to rule the world."

"Bulls-eye!" thought Terra, while controlling her facial expression in order not to betray the accuracy of Mandala's premise. If Ganymede could move identities between bodies, there were no limits to the ways they could exploit that ability. In the case of Marcus Takana, the Director had already conceived a plan to have one of his operatives wind up in Takana's body rather than Ray Mettler, the man who had paid for the privilege. But when Mettler's double cross triggered the switch early, it presented a simpler opportunity to control the power of Takana's office. Just before her death, Terra had been leaning on Mettler to run for President.

But that seemed like eons ago, when she was blind to the depravity of the Director's lust for power and had been willing to act ruthlessly in his service. Now Connor was offering her an opportunity to be on the right side of history.

"If what you're telling me is true," she said at last, putting the knife aside, "what happens next? Where do I fit in?"

"You have access to Ganymede. You can get us past their firewall so we can end this madness once and for all." He raised the left leg of his pants and retrieved a needle like object that had been fastened to the back of his calf. He held it out for her to take.

"This contains a program, a Trojan Horse, that once uploaded will give us access to any system. Upload it into Ganymede's computers and we'll take care of the rest."

She took the module and tucked it away while she let the implications of his words sink in. Was she ready to be a traitor? And what would be the consequences if she were to take part in this venture and dismantle Ganymede's operation? Mandala's objective might be noble, but their means had been deadly before. If she were to succeed, what would become of the pairs of participants already enrolled in the experiment? And what would become of her?

20

WHEN TERRA got back to her car after meeting with Connor and the door lifted up to admit her, she found an intruder in the passenger seat.

"Good morning, Terra," the intruder said.

"Good morning, Ethan. What are you doing here?"

"You were given a mission by the Director. It's been nearly a week. Why haven't you completed it?"

"He's been elusive. We've had no contact since I was at Ganymede."

"Until today," corrected Ethan.

"Yes. Until today."

"So you could have done it today. Or you could have tipped off the authorities at any time."

"I would have had to know where he was to point them in the right direction," Terra replied. "As far as today, I wanted to confirm for myself that he was working for Mandala. And it occurred to me that eliminating him wouldn't eliminate the threat. I have an opportunity to get inside their organization and learn enough to help you dismantle it."

Terra held her breath while Ethan considered her proposition.

"OK. You have another week." Terra had his attention. She'd bought some time. "But if he's not dead or captured by then, I'll take matters in my own hands. And neither of you will like how I handle it. You've seen my work." He opened the door to get out of the car.

"Thanks, Ethan. Don't be a stranger." She smiled as he left the vehicle.

Another week. Not much time to figure out what she needed to do. She wasn't entirely lying about infiltrating Mandala. Before she would do their bidding, she needed to know more about their motives and methods. Connor had bought time with her, too, but she wasn't wholly convinced that his was the more righteous cause.

When she got home, another problem awaited her. She found Macklyn pacing and disturbed. She'd rarely seen her unnerved by anything.

"Someone's been inside," Macklyn said. "In all the time I've lived here, nobody has ever breached our security."

"Is anything missing?" Terra asked.

"Not that I could see. Hardly anything was disturbed. I wouldn't have known that anyone was here if I hadn't seen a strange man leave the building when I got home. I did a UV scan and got traces of footprints that didn't match either of ours. I was sweeping the place for bugs when you got home."

"What did the stranger look like?"

"Dark skin. Asian looking except for his blue eyes. Young."

"Ethan," thought Terra. But she didn't say it aloud. Bugging the apartment would be a logical reason for his intrusion. If he was searching for something, he was careful to put everything back in its place. Ethan was always meticulous. The fragment of footprint Macklyn found was an unusual stroke of luck.

They used all their skills to search for a microphone, camera, or digital device, but found nothing. That didn't mean, however, that they weren't being watched. Ethan was that good. He'd been her mentor, after all.

Even without the transducer, Ganymede had thoroughly infiltrated her life. There was no place left to hide unless she went back on the run and left both Connor and Macklyn behind. And Macklyn was now also in their sights, perhaps to be used to keep Terra in their control. She'd put everyone she cared about in peril.

21

TERRA'S CAR ROLLED into the tunnel toward Ganymede's DC station for the second time, summoned by the Director. This time, Connor's Trojan Horse was embedded in the data port in her thigh. If she could access Ganymede's wireless network with her biometric credentials, the program on the data stick would upload to their system, providing entry for Mandala's hackers. Would she be able to escape detection?

Ethan was again there to greet her when she entered the compound.

"Your week is almost up, Terra," Ethan said. "The Director isn't happy." He left her standing in the middle of the main room and approached the Director's door.

She had only moments. She walked a few steps to the side of a young woman at a workstation. The agent was focused in the space in front of her on a display visible only to her. Terra guessed where the sensor was located on the desk in front of the agent and ran a finger across it. The display became visible. She was in. Now that she was connected, there was nothing more she had to do for the program to load in the system.

Ethan turned and beckoned her to the Director's office. She entered. The Director's face was still in shadows. This time, a few wisps of smoke rose from his mouth when he began to speak.

"You're on pretty thin ice," the Director began. "What's holding things up?"

"You've given me just a week to infiltrate an organization that's eluded you for years," Terra replied. "Isn't that a lot to ask?"

"No matter," said the Director. "It's what I've asked and I expect you to deliver." He brought his wizened hands together on the desk in front of him. Those hands had always held an uncanny power to intimidate her.

"I have a meeting scheduled tomorrow," Terra lied. "That's when he told me I'd meet the others. I'll know more after that."

The Director peered into her eyes. She was dealing with someone trained to expose untruths. Would her skill at creating fabrications match his at detecting them? She stood her ground as more wisps of smoke rose to the ceiling. It was a long wait before he spoke again.

"You have forty-eight hours," he said at last. "Then you will return here to report what you've found. I also expect you to tell me then that you've eliminated Connor Campbell. We will have no further use for him after that."

"I understand," Terra said. She turned to leave. Ethan met her at the door to see her out.

As she stepped back into the tunnel, she heard the voice of a young woman addressing Ethan. "Sir, there seems to have been a breach in the system."

She took off toward her car, looking back as she jumped in to see Ethan running after her. She would need to make the most of her brief head start.

Once out of the tunnel, Terra careened around a corner down a side street, came out to another thoroughfare, then turned down another alleyway. She switched the controls to remote, setting the range as long as possible. With luck, she'd have fifteen miles. She slowed the car, opened the door, jumped out and rolled. As the car sped back up, the wind resistance shut the door. She was out of sight by the time Ethan's car sped by.

Terra had full control of her car's cameras. She had a full 360-degree view as well as the map on the navigation system. She steered it toward the waterfront with Ethan in close pursuit. As the hovercar approached the channel, she swerved onto a pier, traversed its length, and was water bound, headed for the mouth of the Anacostia River and out to the Potomac.

Ethan was closing the gap and hit the water a few hundred yards behind her. By the time they reached the Potomac, he was only a dozen car lengths behind, within laser range. From the rearmost camera, she saw the flash of the laser from the front of Ethan's hovercar. Then the display vanished. He'd hit the mark. The car was now sinking to the bottom of the Potomac, presumably with Terra inside.

It wouldn't be very long, though, before they'd know she was still alive.

22

IT WAS ONLY a matter of time before Ganymede would figure out that Terra hadn't died in her car when it sank in the river. She'd have to abandon the apartment and disappear and would take Macklyn with her. It wouldn't be safe for Macklyn to stay behind since it was already clear that Ganymede knew about both her and their shared abode.

Terra rushed home on foot via back streets to elude detection. She arrived home an hour and a half after leaving the waterfront. She engaged the biometric entry of the apartment. The door opened.

"Macklyn," Terra called upon entering, but there was no response. She was about to call again, but remembered that the place could be under surveillance. She headed for the bedroom.

As she crossed the threshold to the bedroom, her eyes fell upon the crumpled form lying face down beside the bed. She dove to the floor and rolled the body over. Macklyn's breath came in rapid, shallow bursts that barely moved her chest. Her palms were bright red, her eyes open, but unseeing.

Terra rolled her onto her side and swept a finger around the cavity of her mouth. The tiny brown capsule popped out, struck the floor soundlessly and rolled under the bed. Terra rolled her onto her back, shook her, and shouted at her, but she knew she was too late. There was nothing more that she could do to bring Macklyn back. Terra brought her lips to

Macklyn's and felt the last wisps of Macklyn's breath upon her face accompanied by the faint scent of almonds. Then she was dead.

Terra brought her fingers to Macklyn's eyes and closed them, then covered her body with a blanket. Still sobbing, she scanned the room for clues to what led to her friend's death. The government issued poison pill was intended to elude capture by an adversary. Had she been ambushed? There was no sign of a struggle. Or could this have been a deliberate suicide? And if so, what could have pushed this solid rock of a woman over the edge? This room held no answers.

Terra combed the apartment for signs of an intruder. The apartment was clean, but in the world of covert operations, people seldom left traces. Macklyn could have been a victim of Ganymede, but she also had enemies of her own. When Terra had dropped suddenly back into her life, Macklyn still worked for the NSA and never brought her work into their personal life. The less shared, the safer for them both.

Flight would be simpler without Macklyn to slow her down. There was no time to lose before Ganymede would come looking for her. She would be long gone by the time they arrived.

Terra had barely hit the street when a sleek white hovercar drew up beside her. The passenger door opened.

"Get in," said a familiar voice and Terra jumped inside. The car sped away just as Ethan's car pulled up to the front of her building. She breathed deeply and settled back into the seat.

"Nick of time, Connor," she said after catching her breath. "Thanks."

"Thank God you're alive," Connor said. "I thought I'd lost you when your car sank in the river."

Tears began running down Terra's cheeks. She was sobbing too hard to talk. This was the most vulnerable she'd ever been in Connor's presence.

"What's the matter? What happened to you?" Connor asked.

She just shook her head.

"You can tell me about it later," Connor said. "Whatever happened, I wish I'd been there for you. For now, we need to get somewhere safe, to people who can protect us both. It's time you met Mandala."

As the car sped past the city limits and through the Maryland countryside, Terra composed herself and thought about what she would tell Connor about Macklyn. Mandala had provided him some information about her past life when they recruited him, but it would not have included the intimate secrets she'd kept well-hidden even from the NSA and from Ganymede. When they'd first met in DC, all she told Connor was that she was staying with a friend. She didn't elaborate on the nature of that friendship.

They turned down a dirt road and continued for several miles, the hovercar stirring a cloud of dust in its path. The vehicle was designed for slick surfaced roadways, but was versatile enough to handle off road conditions. The car finally slowed as it approached the tall wooden gates of a fortified compound. Armed guards flanked the gates. Terra spotted sharpshooters on the ramparts above.

One of the guards approached as the car came to a stop. After confirming Connor's identity, he raised a hand and the gates parted. Once inside, Terra imagined she'd journeyed a hundred years into the past. They drove past vegetable gardens in neat rows and chickens roaming open fields before coming to a stop in a small village, complete with a pharmacy, general store, and a cafe. The streets were cobblestone, abutting the storefronts without sidewalks.

The people on the streets were clothed mostly in jeans and shirts of denim and cotton, colorfully dyed. There appeared to be families with a scattering of children tagging along with their parents.

Terra had understood Mandala to be a community of hackers. She'd anticipated a technological fortress similar to Ganymede's, populated by agile young agents. This looked more like a movie set for a mid-twentieth century western.

As they approached the cafe, a woman came out to greet them. She appeared fit and trim, about Terra's height, and clothed in white jeans and a blue denim shirt. Her long silver hair was tied back in a ponytail. Her deeply lined face framed a warm and somewhat impish smile. Terra guessed that she was at least seventy. She didn't appear to have indulged in any of the anti-aging technology so prevalent in the culture of the day, at least among the privileged.

"Welcome to Mandala," said the woman, extending her hand to Terra. "I'm Lily."

"Thanks," Terra said, taking Lily's hand.

"Not exactly what you expected, Darlin'?" said Lily with a grin, picking up on Terra's bewildered look.

"That's for sure." Terra found herself smiling despite the tragedy she'd just left behind.

"This is a very special community," Lily said. "Here we believe in the circle of life, in the natural order of things. Aging is a part of life," she continued passing the palm of her hand down over her withered face, "as is death. It's been that way since the beginning of time and it's not up to us to interfere with that."

Terra had learned long ago to pity the elderly. In her culture of youth, she'd shunned contact with those who reminded her of her own mortality. But she felt drawn to this woman's warm demeanor and quiet conviction. She seemed comfortable in her wrinkled skin and at ease with her chosen destiny.

"I can understand if you choose to live this way," Terra said, "but what if others prefer not to age or die? What right do you have to force that upon them?"

"You must understand that all of life is interconnected. We all share the limited resources of the planet," Lily explained. "For some to stay eternally young, it means that others may never get to be. Is that what you would choose? One generation forever?"

Terra felt a twinge of remorse. She'd already enjoyed more than her share of youth and vitality at the expense of others. Petra's life had been sacrificed on her behalf. And in another sense, Macklyn's may have, too. That was a price she'd never intended to pay.

Terra's hand moved unconsciously to her belly. Lily's eyes followed it.

"You see, Darlin'," Lily said without missing a beat, "It's all about new life."

Connor looked at Lily and then at Terra, his eyes wide. Terra met his gaze.

"You're pregnant?" he exclaimed.

She nodded.

"And its…?"

"I hope so. I don't really know. If it happened after I got here, then it's yours. But if it was on Petra's watch, I couldn't say."

"It looks like you two have some things to work out," Lily said. "Meanwhile, we have to figure out how to protect you when you leave here. And leave you must. Once the others become aware of what you are, things could get ugly even after what you've done for us."

"So what exactly did I do?" asked Terra. "What has the program I uploaded made possible?"

"We were able to access Ganymede's database briefly before they discovered the breach and locked us out. We've identified around half of their clients as well as an encryption key they use to communicate with the implanted transducers. Once they figure out we have that, they'll change the key. So we'll need to act fast to take advantage of it. Our people are already on it."

Terra felt a sinking feeling in her gut. She'd been on the other side of an earlier hack that had resulted in a number of their clients dying. Would she now have a part in killing others?

"What are you going to do with it? Are people going to die?"

"That was unfortunate last time," Lily said, "But necessary for the greater good. Please understand that we value life and prefer not to kill needlessly. Back then we needed to send a message and had no other way to do it. We now know how to activate the transducers and initiate the exchanges. We should be able to accomplish that without anybody dying."

Terra considered the implications. Lives weren't going to be lost, but they'd be turned upside down in ways that could destroy relationships and careers. Was changing people's identities in such a drastic way much different from ending their lives?

"Will it be reversible or permanent?" she asked, remembering her experience with Marcus Takana and Ray Mettler when Ganymede managed to return them to their own bodies after Mandala's hack had triggered the exchange.

"We're hoping it will be permanent," Lily said. "Our object is to bring attention to Ganymede's project and to deter others from participating in their experiment. Bringing about these exchanges will be a dramatic way to shine light on what they're doing."

"By destroying people's lives," Terra argued.

"Only changing them, Darlin', in ways they signed up for in the first place, at least for the buyers of the contracts." Lily paused to allow Terra to absorb her words. "And one could argue that for the sellers, they will be far better off than if the exchanges occurred as planned upon their counterparts' deaths."

"Is Mandala playing God with people's lives like this any better than what Ganymede is doing?" Terra wondered. Having lived in another's body for more than a month, she had a personal appreciation for how disorienting that can be. She'd given it little thought in her role as an agent for Ganymede, but the moral implications of both her former role and her new role as saboteur were now crystallizing in her conscience. And this sweet unassuming little old lady wielded stunning power without compunction. There was no turning back.

23

TERRA AWOKE EARLY and arose quietly to keep from awakening Connor, still sleeping in the bed they shared in the cottage provided them by Mandala. She headed across the village square to the cafe in hope of finding superb coffee. Everything in Mandala was naturally sourced and tasted better than most things in the outside world. It was a beautiful morning, the sunrise painting scarlet and gold across the horizon.

Just as she was about to enter the cafe, she felt a stinging pain between her shoulder blades, then saw a stone the size of a chestnut hit the ground at her feet.

"She's one of them!" shouted a man behind her. She whirled to see him preparing to throw another stone. "She's one of their freaks. She doesn't belong here."

Suddenly a crowd had formed and stones fell like hail from all directions. She looked around at their faces, which were contorted with rage. There would be no reasoning with this mob.

Terra took off straight through the middle of the crowd for the open space between her and the walls of the compound. The stones stung her from all directions. But Petra's body, like hers, was exceptionally strong and fast. In moments, she'd broken free of the crowd and was headed for the wall, where there were ladders to the ramparts for the compound's defenders. She scrambled up the nearest ladder, ran a few steps along the walkway at the top, and hurled herself over the razor wire.

She hit the ground hard at the end of a long drop, went into a forward roll, and sprang to her feet. Petra's body served her well. She was uninjured. As she sprinted for the edge of the woods, she heard gunshots behind her. Bullets ricocheted off the ground by her feet. For an organization that employed state of the art digital skills in their work, Mandala was remarkably old school in its style of living and fighting.

Once she was in the trees, the shooting stopped. They'd be in pursuit soon enough, but she had time to catch her breath and plan her next moves. She had no weapons, no transportation, and no way to communicate with Connor, who was still behind the walls of the compound.

As she sat on the ground with her back against a tree, she heard rustling nearby, then the sharp sound of a breaking twig. She dove to the ground just as a laser burned a hole through the tree where her head had been. As she rolled into cover, she caught a glimpse of her new adversary. It was Ethan.

She broke into a zigzag run among the trees. She was trapped. There was nowhere left to hide and still no weapon. Ethan's weapon was far deadlier than the rifles of Mandala. Unlike bullets, his laser could penetrate tree trunks.

Terra's broken-field flight pattern took her randomly through the woods until she emerged into the open space that faced the compound. Ethan appeared at the edge of the woods not fifty yards distant, his weapon pointed straight at her. It was all over, and she hadn't another life to spare.

She heard the crack of a gunshot and Ethan fell to the ground, writhing. Another shot and he was still. Terra looked up to the ramparts where Lily brandished a rifle, waving her off. The other shooters had stood down.

Terra ran to Ethan and confirmed that he was dead. She took his weapon and used the laser to slice off the tip of a forefinger. She had no idea whether Lily had been able to rein in the mob or if they'd be after her again. She'd still have to run.

She cut through the woods to the road that led to the compound. Ethan's car sat at the road's edge a short sprint away. When she reached it, she touched the severed fingertip to the door. It lifted open. When she placed it on the sensor on the dashboard, the door closed, the car rose off the ground and sped down the road.

Terra realized that she'd be able to spoof Ethan's identity with his DNA for a very short time before Ganymede would know that he was dead and take control of the car. For all she knew, they might already know. It took only a few minutes to speed back to civilization. She got out by the side of a highway and sent the car crashing into an abutment. With luck, they'd assume that he died in the crash. If they'd figured out that she'd been driving, they might assume that she'd been the one to die. Even better luck.

Connor would know that Terra was the last person to drive Ethan's car. By destroying it she risked him thinking she was dead. They were once again separated and out of touch. She wondered if she would ever see him again.

24

BY THE TIME SHE'D FOUND a place to stay, the effects of Mandala's hack were already widespread. A nationwide epidemic was reported of Capgras Syndrome, a rare mental condition in which people believed that others close to them had been replaced by exact doubles. Dozens of people had been admitted to the scant psychiatric hospital beds that still existed.

Even more remarkable was that some of the alleged doubles seemed to share the delusion, a bizarre form of folie à deux. They claimed that their consciousness and their identities had been transferred from their original bodies. When asked about how that could have happened, some became evasive, while others claimed that it was the result of a top-secret government project to confer immortality upon a select few. Such conspiracy theories were a garden variety element of paranoid delusions. They'd mean nothing to the treating professionals unless they compared details among cases that were scattered in hospitals all over the map.

One such case had been admitted to a hospital in Virginia, not far from where Terra was staying. A husband and wife had been admitted together, the husband claiming that his wife was an imposter and the wife acknowledging that she wasn't who she appeared to be. To complicate matters further, the woman was a Senator of considerable prominence and an heiress to a sizeable fortune. Her apparent illness was turning into a huge scandal that was likely to end her political career.

With her skills as a covert operative, it was child's play for Terra to fabricate credentials for a new identity as an expert psychiatric consultant and gain access to this couple. Until she was in their presence, however, she wasn't sure what she was going to do with this opportunity. While exposing Ganymede seemed like a worthwhile objective, it would need to be done in a convincing way in order to mobilize forces against them. And if there were any possibility remaining of reversing the exchanges, exposing Ganymede and forcing them to cover their tracks might shut that off forever.

Terra asked to meet the woman first. The patient was introduced to her as Carrie.

"I'm Dr. Froming," Terra introduced herself, extending her hand. "I'm here to help figure out what happened to you."

Carrie was a diminutive wisp of a woman, a head shorter than Terra, frail and on the cusp between middle aged and elderly. Most of the people who'd acknowledged their unusual condition and been hospitalized with their partners were similarly old. They had the least to lose by coming out publicly, while those who had migrated to younger bodies had more reason to be secretive.

"This wasn't supposed to happen," said the woman, wringing her hands. "I had a life. I was supposed to stay young indefinitely. What am I supposed to do with this pathetic body? It hurts everywhere."

"Can we go back to the beginning?" said Terra, still thinking about ways to leverage her position. "What was supposed to happen?"

"They told me I'd live for a long time," said the woman. "Eventually someone would die and take my body, and then my life would be over. But that was supposed to be it. An ending. Oblivion. Not purgatory in an aging body."

"Who promised you these things?" asked Terra.

"It was a young man," said the woman. "He showed up one day out of the blue when my life was going down the drain. He promised me unimaginable wealth and eternal youth in exchange for giving up my body whenever some unnamed person died. This must be who it was." She passed her hand down over her torso. "And I guess she's in my body now."

"What did he look like?"

The woman described Ethan in precise detail. She was one of his clients.

"So tell me," Terra asked next. "Who are you really?"

"My name is Magic Skylark," said the woman. "When I told them that was my name, they could barely hide their amusement. It sounded as fantastic as the rest of the story I was telling. But that's really my name. I'm native American."

The irony wasn't lost on Terra. A woman claiming to be someone else named Magic of all things would seem highly improbable to the uninitiated. It had served to convince them all the more that she was crazy.

"You must think I'm crazy, too," said the woman, misreading the thoughts behind Terra's expression. Terra took her by both hands and looked into her eyes.

"What if I told you that I believed you?" Terra said, mustering her most empathetic smile.

"Then I'd say you were lying. Hell, if I were in your position, I wouldn't believe me either."

"Was the young man's name Ethan...the one who got you into this?"

"Yes, it was." Her expression brightened for a moment, then dissolved back into a frown. "But of course you read that in my record. I told them his name and they must have written it down."

"Magic," Terra said next, "if I can call you that. Where are you from?"

"Florida, Pensacola originally before it got washed away. Then I moved to Atlanta." Her voice sounded tentatively hopeful. "Dr. Froming, I had a life, a family. I have a son. He's only six. I just want to see him again."

"We need to find your family, then," Terra said. "Can you help me do that?"

"Yes, yes," the woman almost shouted. "I'll do whatever you need. Then you really do believe me?"

"I do." As she spoke, Terra reached behind the woman's right ear, her finger finding the tiny transducer that had escaped the examining hands of the admitting doctor. It rolled slightly beneath the skin.

Touching the device convinced Magic that Terra believed her. She placed her withered hand over Terra's, which still rested upon her face.

"Thank you," she said, tears welling in her eyes. "Thank you for saving my life."

"I can't get you out of here just yet," Terra said. "You'll need to be patient. It will take some time to convince others that your story is true."

Terra knew what she had to do next. She would find Magic Skylark and convince her to go public with her situation. Only with both sides of this contract cooperating to tell their stories would the world believe what Ganymede had wrought.

25

TERRA ARRIVED in Buckhead, a tony suburb on the northern edge of Atlanta, and looked for the address that Magic had provided her. She found an attractive two-story home with a stone front that was designed to look old, but which had been built less than five years earlier. A mailbox by the road bore the name Skylark, but it was just a prop to make the house appear dated. Mail hadn't been delivered for decades.

She ascended the five steps to the front door and knocked. There was no answer. She knocked again and waited. The door finally opened a crack and a young woman's head peered through the crack.

"Magic Skylark?" asked Terra.

"Who wants to know?" replied the woman.

"My name is Dr. Froming. I'm a psychiatrist. I've just come from seeing Carrie Samuelson in a hospital in Virginia."

The woman's eyes grew wide. She began to shake.

"Come in," she said. "You have my attention."

Terra entered to find a warmly decorated home ablaze with color. Turquoise and coral dominated the color scheme of the upholstery and the abundant art on the wall. Toys littered the floor. A child's head peered shyly from around a door jamb.

The woman standing before her was strikingly handsome, tall and svelte. The dress she wore clung flatteringly to the natural curves of her body. The olive skin of her face was framed in black hair and set off ebony eyes that reminded Terra of Macklyn's. She pushed down the grief in order to stay focused on her task.

The woman nodded in the direction of the child.

"He doesn't know," she said, "but you can tell he has an idea that something's wrong. He keeps his distance most of the time and stares at me from across the room. And he hasn't been sleeping. He calls out with nightmares all night. His father goes to him, but can hardly soothe him. He needs his mother."

"Does his father know?" asked Terra.

"He has a pretty good idea. He came on to me last night and was upset when I rebuffed him. I've not had sex in years and have been comfortable with that. I'm not ready to start again now and certainly not with a stranger."

"Have you talked about it?"

"He hasn't confronted me directly. I think with everything in the news feeds about people getting hospitalized with delusions he's afraid to say something that might get him locked up." She sighed deeply and sank back into a chair. "You know, this is a nightmare for everyone involved."

"So you're not happy?"

"How can I be happy?"

"You have a new life in a vital new body. You're in the prime of health and pain free. Why shouldn't you be happy?"

"Because it's not my life. It's someone else's. I don't belong here. And I have unfinished work in my career. I was working on crucial legislation when this mess disrupted everything. I need to go back."

"I don't know if that will be possible, Carrie," said Terra, sitting down beside her, "but I'll do what I can. There may be something you can do to help."

"Who are you, anyway?" the woman asked. "You don't sound like a doctor. How did you figure out who I am?"

"My name is Terra. I once worked for them, doing the same thing that Ethan did with you. I set up contracts and monitored the progress of my clients. What happened to me is a long story that we don't have time for now. I just know that this whole business needs to stop."

"How can I help?"

"I want you go public...to tell the world what happened to you and what a disaster it's turned out to be," Terra said. "We need to reach out to as many others as possible and convince them to terminate their contracts."

"How can they do that?"

"By having their transducers removed. Without the transducers, the exchanges can't take place."

"If only it weren't too late for me. I'd give anything to have my own life back, to live it out, however briefly, and to die in my own skin."

Carrie's story was on the UDB by nightfall. It set off a firestorm of related stories as others came out from the shadows with their own stories. The teams of professionals treating the hospitalized patients turned their focus from treating a delusion to addressing the trauma of undergoing a radical change of identity. Treatment teams swooped down on the families of those affected to help deal with their adjustment to these changes.

Ganymede was now in the public eye. While none of the victims knew exactly who was responsible for their predicament, they all told the media similar stories of being approached by agents of a mysterious organization that dabbled in immortality. Some of the clients who hadn't been involved in the hack began showing up at surgical centers to have their transducers extracted. Terra knew that the numbers of people going public were just the tip of the iceberg of all the people involved in Ganymede's web. And even without the transducers, who knew what the nanoparticle networks in the brains of the participants, and in her brain, might do over time.

One other consequence of Carrie Samuelson's disclosure was flagging Terra's presence in Atlanta. She hoped that it would lead Connor back to her, but it also risked exposing her location to Ganymede.

Connor found her first. He showed up in the middle of the night and spirited her out of the city. By morning they were in a cabin high in the Smoky Mountains north of Gatlinburg, sitting by a fire. The glow of the fire in Connor's eyes warmed her more than the fire itself. The feeling of his lips upon hers helped her forget for just a moment how much she missed Macklyn.

Terra was also happy to see Connor because of his connection with Mandala. Since they'd made the exchanges a one-way process by shutting down the transducers, they were also the only ones able to reactivate them. If Ganymede had known how to do that, they would have already done it. Now that Mandala had accomplished the main goal of their intervention, there was little to prevent them from undoing it.

"Was Lily planning to reverse the exchanges?" Terra asked Connor as they lay in bed after making love.

"I don't think so," Connor replied. "She wanted to make an example of them...a lasting impression."

"Seems like they've already accomplished that. What good can come of making all these people go on suffering?"

"As you well know," Connor reminded her, "the people of Mandala aren't entirely rational. You saw how they attacked you. Lily's command of the group is fragile. I think she might agree with you, but she doesn't have the last word."

"I saw that little boy and thought about my own child...our child." She put his hand on her belly and looked into his eyes. "There must be something we can do."

Connor rolled her onto her side, snuggled into her from behind, and kissed her softly on the neck. He had nothing more to say.

26

TERRA AWOKE in Connor's arms as the first morning light filtered through the trees into their bedroom window. She inhaled deeply the combined aromas of the log cabin, pine needles, and mountain air. It was hard to imagine in this peaceful retreat the crisis still raging that they'd left behind. She wished that they could stay there together forever.

She rummaged through the cupboard in the kitchen and found a bag of fresh coffee and a French press. The smell of the coffee filled the room by the time Connor joined her at the table. She'd taken her first sip when the stillness was interrupted by a sharp rapping on the door.

Connor went to the door, opened it a crack, and peered outside to see a tall man in a park ranger's uniform, his empty hands by his sides. Connor opened the door wider.

"Morning, Folks," said the man. "Just making the rounds to pass along some safety tips during your stay." As he spoke, he pushed the door fully open, giving him a clear view of the kitchen. He looked straight at Terra.

"A couple of bears have been spotted around the camp," he continued. "It's important not to leave any food accessible outside the cabin. And you shouldn't carry anything edible on your person." His gaze lingered on Terra long enough to make her uncomfortable.

"Thank you," she said. "Is there anything else?"

"That's all. Just remember that this is their home. Enjoy your stay." He turned and walked away.

Terra listened for the sound of a vehicle departing, but heard neither the closing of a door nor the telltale sound of a hovercar lifting off the ground. As she listened, she thought she heard muffled footsteps moving toward the rear of the cabin. Something was off. Then, hovering above the fresh scent of mountain air was the faint, pungent smell of gasoline.

"Whoosh!" The cabin was suddenly encircled in flames that quickly ignited its wooden walls and licked the openings at the kitchen windows.

Connor instinctively threw open the kitchen door. The flames bursting through the opening brushed him back, singeing his clothes. Terra sprang from her chair, in one motion kicking the door shut with her foot and knocking Connor to the floor. She heard the door latch. The flames momentarily abandoned the windows as the room began to fill with smoke.

"Stay low and follow me," she said and began crawling toward the bedroom. She snatched the vintage fire extinguisher she'd spotted in the kitchen while making coffee and prayed that it was still charged. Once Connor was past the bedroom door, she kicked it shut, pulled bedding from the bed and crammed it against the opening at the bottom of the door.

The smoke above their heads was thinner than the smoke they'd left behind in the kitchen, which was apparently the epicenter of the fire. Flames were beginning to make their way along the walls toward the bedroom windows. She motioned Connor toward the furthest window, raised the fire extinguisher, and began spraying down the walls with foam, creating a perimeter around the window.

"Get ready to jump," she commanded, striking the base of the window frame with the heavy butt of the extinguisher. The window gave way. "Now!" she yelled, propelling him toward the opening by the seat of his pants.

Connor flew cleanly through the window and rolled as he hit the ground on the other side. Terra followed instants later as the flames engulfed the window. They both kept rolling away from the cabin as the flames exploded upward to consume it.

Terra's body bore the brunt of the fire. There were severe enough burns on her arms and face that Connor could smell the burning flesh. His horrified expression alerted Terra to the severity of wounds that were unaccompanied by pain.

"I'll be OK," she reassured him, mustering a weak smile. "I have remarkable powers of healing."

The sound of a branch cracking in the distance reminded them that they were still under attack. The ranger, or whoever he was, had clearly meant to kill them. He was still nearby and likely to try again. They began to run in the opposite direction from the sound. She listened for the sound of gunshots, but looked back in time to see a flash of blue light from the distance burn a hole through Connor's left shoulder. He went down. Her heart sank.

"Laser gun," she thought. "Ganymede's found us."

Her first impulse was to run to Connor, but realized that if she did so they were both dead. She circled around, then used her extraordinary agility to scramble up into the canopy of trees and waited. The ranger scoured the area beneath her, retracing his steps several times before giving up. She watched him withdraw to his waiting vehicle, get inside, and appear to communicate with someone for a minute or two before driving away.

Terra descended to the forest floor and ran as fast as she could to the spot where Connor had fallen. When she got there, it was empty. No Connor. She could see by the matted ground cover and puddle of blood that she was in the right place.

"Connor," she yelled out. "He's gone. You can come out now." There was no response. From the severity of his wound and the stillness of his body where he'd hit the ground, she realized that he couldn't possibly have made it more than a hundred feet from the spot, especially with their adversary prowling the area. His body, dead or alive, had vanished into thin air. She was alone once more.

27

THE SOUND OF BRANCHES crashing to the ground and the smell of smoke alerted Terra to the march of the forest fire across the space between her and the cabin. The raging fire had already destroyed the vehicle they'd driven to the forest. She could feel the heat of the fire at her back and broke into a run. The fire gained on her. As the heat intensified at her back, she stumbled and rolled down an embankment to the edge of a creek. She scrambled into the water.

The narrow stream would provide a temporary firebreak, but she was under no illusion that it would protect her from the fire for long. She swam downstream a few hundred yards and emerged on the other side just wide of the fire's path. As she ran, she heard another sound above her head, like a swarm of bees. She looked up to see a flotilla of half a dozen drones passing just overhead.

"Ganymede," she thought, and prepared for the worst. There would be no escaping their aerial pursuit. But the drones continued past her toward the fire. She turned to see a deluge of water pour from the aircraft, followed by rising steam from the quenching flames. The advance of the fire was contained for the moment, buying her time, but it was far from extinguished.

Now she became aware that she wasn't alone in her flight from the fire. Not fifty feet downwind was a pair of black bears fleeing in a path parallel to hers. She saw them sniff the air and realized that they'd picked up her scent, driven by the wind and magnified by the drifting smoke, but escaping the fire would still take priority over pursuing prey. If they ever got beyond the fire's reach, however, that equation would change in a flash. All she could do now was keep running.

A second wave of drones passed overhead and dumped their loads of water on the fire. The onset was slowed sufficiently that she could no longer feel the heat at her back. She stopped running long enough to catch her breath, then saw the pair of predators turn in her direction. As fast as her genetically modified body could run, she couldn't outrun these animals.

Terra spotted a boulder around twenty feet away and sprang for it, scooping a branch in each hand along the way. She leaped to the surface of the rock and turned to face the attacking bears, stretching to full height with her arms and the branches above her head. She made a menacing face and growled loudly. The animals stopped in their tracks. One of them turned and trotted into the brush, but the other stood his ground, then leaped straight at her. She snapped one of the branches, striking the bear square on the nose. The huge animal whimpered, then lumbered off.

Terra waited nearly ten minutes before abandoning her perch atop the boulder. As she began to make her way cautiously through the woods, she wondered how she'd get back to civilization. She was many miles from the nearest village and had no food, water, weapon, or means of communication. Even if she had a way to call for help, she had no idea whom to call that she could trust. With both Macklyn and Connor gone, she had more chance of being found by an adversary than by a friend. She walked until dark in the direction she believed would lead out of the woods, then collapsed in exhaustion in a thicket by a creek. The burbling of the water flowing over the rock bed lulled her to sleep.

Terra awoke at daybreak to the sound of a gasoline engine and the creaking sounds of an aging vehicle rol ing on uneven ground. She peered through the branches just as the jeep rolled past. A shotgun protruding from the passenger side pointed directly at her. She ducked down and waited for the gunshot. It never came.

The jeep pulled up around fifty feet away and the engine stopped. She heard a door shut, then footsteps. When she looked in the direction of the footsteps, she saw the shotgun again, now slung across the back of the intruder.

"You can come out now, Darlin'," said a familiar female voice. "The cavalry's here to save your sorry ass."

Terra emerged from her hiding place and Lily turned to face her.

"You and Connor have gotten yourselves in quite a fix," Lily said. "You're lucky I found you first."

"Then you have Connor? He's alive?" asked Terra, her heart filling with hope.

"Unfortunately, no," answered Lily shaking her head. "Connor's alive, but he's been captured. Ganymede's got him."

"How do you know?"

"They've been in touch, making demands. They're keeping him as a hostage."

"What do they want?"

"They want us to undo what we've done, to reverse the exchanges."

"So why not give them what they want? You've made your statement. You've had your exposure. What do you have to lose now?"

"It's not that simple, Darlin'," said Lily. "Connor's not the first of our people they've captured. After the first hack, they snatched one of our programmers and forced her to reverse the exchanges among the survivors. Once she gave them what they wanted, they killed her."

Terra hadn't been aware of the kidnapping or murder at the time of the earlier hack. Now she knew how Ganymede had managed to put Marcus and Ray back where they belonged. She shuddered to realize she'd been a part of it.

"So you're afraid that once they get what they want, they'll kill him anyway?"

"You can count on it, seein' who he is."

"I don't understand."

"Then I guess he hasn't told you the whole truth," Lily said, putting both hands on Terra's shoulders. "Connor's not just a soldier. He's the leader of our ragtag band...and he's my son."

A rush of blood turned Terra's face almost as red as her hair. The whole truth? He hadn't told her any of the truth. Not that he was responsible for the hack that switched Magic Skylark for Carrie Samuelson and not that he, not Lily, had the ultimate authority to undo the damage. She'd trusted him and he'd used her. Maybe he deserved whatever Ganymede had in store for him.

"We need your help, Darlin'," said Lily. "We need you to help us rescue my son."

Terra's emotions were in a tangle. She was furious at Connor for deceiving her. It even flashed through her mind just for a moment that he could have been responsible for Macklyn's death. But hearing that he was alive had sent a thrill through her. She still longed to be with him. And when Lily appealed for her help rescuing her child, she thought about the life growing within her and what she'd be willing to do to protect the life of that child, her child, Connor's child.

"OK," Terra said at last. "What happens next?"

28

ONCE THEY EMERGED from the cover of the forest, they were met by a helicopter that snatched the jeep from the ground with a sling and drew it up into its hold. When the cargo was secured, the main rotor shifted to a forward position and the aircraft sped to a landing strip in the Maryland countryside. They were met by a contingent from Mandala, who escorted them to the compound.

"Don't worry, Darlin'," Lily reassured her, "They'll behave themselves this time. Connor gave them quite a dressing down after they attacked you. And they want Connor back as much as we do. They know you're here to help."

Terra still wasn't sure how much she wanted Connor back. She had no idea whether he could be trusted and whether or not she'd ever again be willing to let her guard down. If she ever did see him again, he'd have to answer to her for his betrayal and might just wish she'd left him with Ganymede.

She felt her body tense as the compound came into view and she remembered the stoning within its walls. It was hard to accept that those same walls now provided safety and that the people within were her allies.

Once inside, she was treated like an honored guest. She was provided a delectable meal of freshly harvested vegetables and an omelet from free range heirloom chickens raised on site. It was accompanied by a mellow Pinot Noir, a rare mid-century luxury, and followed by one of the silkiest cups of coffee she'd ever had. By the end of the meal, she was almost ready to forget that they'd tried to kill her not so long ago.

That evening, she met with Lily and a handful of the elders of the community to plan a strategy for rescuing Connor. All they had going for them was Terra knowing the location of the entrance to Ganymede's base. She no longer had operable biometric credentials. Gaining entry to the most secretive organization within the Commonwealth's intelligence network would be a formidable challenge.

Without any solutions in sight, they adjourned for the night. Terra was shown to the same cottage that she'd shared with Connor on her previous visit. As much as her adrenaline had been flowing until then, she was now completely drained and ready to sleep. Perhaps her thinking would be clearer in the morning.

When she'd stripped off what remained of her clothing and washed the soot from her body, her skin was still reddened in a few places, but the second and third degree burns had all but healed. Petra's body was proving as strong and durable as the one she'd left behind. It would take another straight shot to the head or heart to kill her.

Connor's body was another story. His shoulder wound from the laser gun was grave and potentially life-threatening. Ganymede's ransom demand notwithstanding, she had no way at this point to be certain that he was still alive.

As Terra began drifting off to sleep, the walls of the cottage dissolved around her and she was back in the massive bedroom of Petra's mansion, sitting astride Connor on the enormous round bed. As the rhythm of her hips rising and falling intensified and her breathing became more rapid, the sound of a garage door opening stopped her just short of climax. They fell still and listened for the sounds of the hovercar settling to the garage floor and the door rolling shut. Connor sprang for the bedroom door, clothes in hand.

She heard the front door slam shut, followed almost immediately by the sound of another door closing, then footsteps accelerating to a run, then bounding up the stairs to the bedroom.

By the time Kresky entered the bedroom, Petra was dressed, but the bedclothes were still disheveled. Kresky's muscles rippled with the rage running through his body.

"What the hell's going on here?" boomed Kresky. "What's he doing here?"

"Who?" she replied.

"Connor. That's who. I can tell he was here. I heard him running out the front door. He has no business being here when I'm not here."

"He's doing his work," she lied. "He came to interview me...to get some background about us for your biography."

"In the bedroom? He has no business in our bedroom!"

"He wasn't in the bedroom. We met in the study. I came up here when we were done."

The blow from the back of his hand came without warning and knocked her face down on the bed. Then he was upon her, one hand pulling her head back by the hair and the other grasping her by the crotch.

"You better not be lying," he growled. "Remember that you're mine and only mine, bought and paid for. If I catch you with him or any other man, I'll kill you both." He pushed her face into the bed so that she could hardly breathe and clenched his other hand until the pain between her legs shot into her navel. Then he left the bedroom and slammed the door hard enough to rattle the windows.

"This has to stop," she thought, "even if I have to kill him."

The searing pain had burst the portal to Petra's past wide open. It wasn't the first time Kresky had beaten her. And it wasn't always out of jealousy. She'd been battered and jerked around for years. Even at the beginning of their marriage, she'd never felt loved. She'd only been a sex object, a possession, a trophy. The only times she felt safe in his presence was when they sometimes shared tea together in the garden. In the garden, he was civilized, even respectful. But even then, she despised him and fantasized about spiking his tea with something slowly lethal.

Was it just a fantasy or had she really done it? That part of her memory was still shrouded in obscurity. And what about Connor? Was he jealous enough or hateful enough to have murdered Kresky or would that have crippled the mission that had brought him into their lives? The more she learned about Connor, the more she appreciated his potential for treachery and deceit.

Terra heard a rapping on the door and opened her eyes. It was morning and the sun was already high. The rapping repeated, harder with more insistence. The door opened a crack.

"Terra, Darlin', rise and shine. It's another day and we've got news." She'd found Lily's familiarity charming at first, but it was starting to cloy.

"Give me a minute," Terra replied. "I'll be right out."

With a fragrant cup of Mandala's special coffee in her hands, Terra watched Lily's animated face and awaited the news.

"They want to deal," Lily said. "And I think we can make it work and get him back."

"That solves the problem of breaking into Ganymede, but what's changed? Why don't you still think they'll kill him?"

"They've offered to set up a meeting...someplace public where we can make an exchange. They finally figured out that Connor couldn't give them the code they need to reverse the exchanges. He's no engineer. He's just a strategist. They're desperate to get that code. We hand them the drive. They validate the content and give us Connor."

"What's to stop them from killing us all before we leave?" asked Terra.

"Well, first of all, 'we' is you. And 'they' will be just one agent...someone of value that they won't want to put at risk. The meeting place will be at the west end of the reflecting pool opposite the Lincoln Memorial, way out in the open at noon. Even Ganymede wouldn't risk killing bystanders or damaging national treasures in a firefight. By the time you and Connor get to the perimeter, we'll be there to get you."

"Not exactly a slam dunk," said Terra. "I can think of a hundred ways this could go wrong. How will they validate the code?"

"They'll try it on a pair of clients in their custody. They'll know right away if it works. Look," Lily continued, "we don't have a lot of options. They hold most of the cards. If we ever hope to see Connor alive, this is our only chance."

Terra had to agree. She would have the advantage of her extraordinary strength and speed, unless they pitted her against someone with similar attributes. In her experience, Ethan had been the closest to her match of all the agents in Ganymede. And Ethan was dead. For her, the opportunity to confront Connor about his lies and to reach a resolution, one way or another, about their relationship was worth the risk she was about to take.

29

TERRA DONNED a skintight jumpsuit designed for speed and covered it with an olive-green tunic that concealed her body from her neck to her ankles. She trimmed off the bulk of her already lush red hair, wrapping the rest tightly in a headscarf and making sure that no strand peeked out. Cobalt mirrored sunglasses completed her disguise. She inserted the memory needle into the tiny compartment on the top edge of her shoe that was designed to hold it.

Lily drove Terra to downtown DC, letting her out at the corner of 19th and C Streets. She melted into the foot traffic headed for the National Mall, wending her way unnoticed to the Reflecting Pool. She took a position near the northwest corner of the pool and watched the movement of the crowd.

A few minutes later, she spotted a pair of men approaching from the southwest. As they got closer, she identified one of them as Connor. He was accompanied by a taller, thin man wearing a hat and sunglasses that obscured his face. When they reached the corner of the pool opposite her, she removed the scarf. The man acknowledged her by removing his hat. She recognized the forest ranger that had tried to kill them.

"Hello, Terra," said the man. "We meet again." The voice was missing the backwoods dialect he'd feigned in the woods. Now there was something very familiar about the cadence of his speech that sent a chill down her spine.

"Ethan!" she exclaimed. "So it's you."

"You didn't think you had a corner on coming back from the dead, did you?" he taunted. "I was partial to my old body, though. I still owe you one for destroying it."

"I'm not the one who shot you."

"Maybe not, but it was done on your behalf, which is pretty much the same. But don't worry, today's not my day for revenge. We'll get to that another day."

Connor stood quietly throughout this exchange. He seemed almost in a trance. While he looked like Connor, Terra began to doubt his identity. She knew Ganymede to have extraordinary skill at creating imposters. She removed her glasses and peered into his glazed eyes.

"Talk to me," she demanded.

"I'm sorry," Connor said in a voice that sounded like he was talking through quicksand. "I screwed up." The cadence was slow and mechanical, but the voice was unmistakably Connor's. Drugged, but still Connor.

"Let's get on with it, Terra," said Ethan. "Give me the code."

She hesitated, doubt still lingering, but decided that she had more to lose by reneging than by giving up Mandala's code. On this score, at least, her interests and Ganymede's were accordant. They both wanted to put things back the way they were before the exchanges.

She reached down, extracted the memory stick from her shoe, and handed it to Ethan. At the same time, she took Connor by the hand and drew him to her side, then scanned him for electronic bugs, trackers, and booby traps. He was clean.

"Hold on, Terra," Ethan said. "You're not going anywhere until I validate the code." He drew a module from his pocket and inserted the needle into a port. The module lit up momentarily, then went dark.

"Now we wait," Ethan said.

While they waited, Terra stripped off the tunic and folded it in a pile at her feet. If she needed to make a fast retreat, she preferred to be unencumbered. In his drugged state, however, Connor would likely have difficulty keeping up, a handicap she hadn't anticipated.

The module vibrated and lit up again. Ethan glanced at the screen, then back at Terra and Connor.

"The code worked," he said. "You're free to go. Until next time, then, Terra," he added with a menacing grin. "I'm not finished with you yet."

Terra and Connor melted back into the crowd and across Constitution Avenue. Lily's car was waiting where she'd let her off. Terra pushed Connor into the back seat and got in beside him. The car lurched forward and sped toward the Maryland countryside and Mandala.

"He doesn't look so good," Lily said once they were underway. "What's wrong with him?"

"Drugged. I guess to prevent us from running."

"I don't like it," said Lily. "He looks like he's been brainwashed."

That had already crossed Terra's mind. Connor had been in Ganymede's hands long enough for them to perpetrate all manner of mischief on his body and mind. Having been on the other side, she was familiar with their capabilities. But there was nothing left to do but be vigilant until his head was clear enough to assess his state of mind.

The gates of the stockade opened upon their approach. Terra glanced at Connor now sleeping beside her. She felt an involuntary twinge in her gut, a feeling that usually meant danger. She was about to enter the bosom of Mandala for a third time.

30

BACK IN THE COTTAGE, Terra stripped off Connor's clothes and gave him a sponge bath. He smelled like he hadn't been bathed since he was captured in the forest. She could still smell smoke on his clothes and in his hair, mixed with the rank odor of old sweat.

Washing him this way evoked unexpected feelings of intimacy and affection. As angry as she'd been with him, she found herself tending him gently, lovingly. She squeezed water from the washcloth as one would upon a child, then drew the tail of the cloth down the length of his body in a swirling pattern. As the cloth passed over his genitals, his penis began to stiffen and his eyes opened halfway. He looked up at her and smiled, then drifted back to sleep. She slid a soapy hand around his penis and lifted it briefly to her lips, then rinsed him and patted him dry.

She had no idea what was in store when the drugs wore off. She wasn't even close to ready to forgive him. There was going to be a horrible fight before there would be any chance to clear the air. But for now, he was helpless in her care. And she appreciated this peaceful interlude before the next act began.

Before she dressed him for bed, Terra examined Connor's body in minute detail for any signs of trauma or tampering. The only wound she found was the one in his shoulder where Ethan had shot him with the laser gun. A single stitch had been placed to close the entry wound, which was

133

healing nicely. The exit wound was also nearly closed. As an afterthought, she ran her fingers over the notches behind his earlobes, probing for transducers. She found none.

Terra awoke the next morning just before dawn to find Connor gone. She looked at the rumpled bedding next to her, then went to the closet. His shoes and one set of his clothes were gone. She dressed and headed to the cafe where she found Connor and Lily sitting together deep in conversation.

They both looked up when the door shut behind her. Connor gave her a chastened smile that told her that Lily must have brought him up to speed about what Terra knew.

"Our boy's back among the living," Lily said, flashing a grin. "A bit the worse for wear, but definitely himself."

Terra was speechless. She'd imagined their reunion and had every intention to hold his feet to the fire for having deceived her, but the image from the night before of him helpless and naked intruded, softening her heart. She shook her head and took a seat at the table.

"I guess you kids have some things to talk about," Lily said, rising from the table. "Just try to play nice."

Terra just looked at Connor and waited for him to speak.

"I'd understand completely if you never trusted me again," he began. "There's no excuse for having kept you in the dark for so long."

That was enough for Terra to connect with the anger she'd kept inside. She felt it bubbling up with a head of pressure behind it.

"I did trust you," she almost shouted. "I put my life on the line for you and it damn near got me killed!"

"And I'm truly sorry for that. I wish I could go back and do it differently. But I was afraid that if you knew the whole truth...who I am and what I've been responsible for, you'd have shut me out a long time ago."

"You're probably right," Terra said. "I don't agree with most of what you and Mandala have done. You've been reckless and indifferent to the destruction you've inflicted upon innocent lives."

"I understand how you feel, but once you spend some time here and get to know our community, you might begin to appreciate what drives us."

Terra desperately wanted to be able to forgive him, but it would take a huge leap of faith. On the other hand, she'd once allowed herself to be the instrument of a pernicious organization that may have aspired to nothing less than world domination. And she'd been ruthless in executing her role. She'd been Ethan's protégé and had learned her lessons well. As despicable as Ethan had proven to be, she'd once been his match. Perhaps the path to forgiveness for Connor would start by finding a way to forgive herself.

She decided to stay at Mandala, at least for a while. She had nowhere else to go. Once she allowed herself to settle into the tempo of the community, she discovered what a special place it was...an odd paradox of a community pursuing its mission by means of its singular technical expertise while living a simple, wholesome lifestyle close to nature.

Connor introduced her to the wonders of nineteenth century farming and to the delights of the natural fruits of its methods. He participated in the work alongside the others while Terra watched and learned, then dove in with gusto. She helped collect eggs and milked cows and goats by hand. She was like a child discovering the world for the first time.

In their day to day life in their relationships with one another, Connor's people were gentle and charitable. It was only when they interacted with an outside world hostile to their values that they became rigid and bellicose, as Terra had experienced on her first visit to Mandala.

The community's reverence for Connor and for Lily became increasingly evident during her time there. Connor knew every citizen by name, greeting them warmly and showing a genuine interest in their lives and well-being. They, in turn, went out of their way to provide him tokens of their esteem and respect. Terra hadn't encountered such a noble appearing presence since Marcus Takana became Minister of Discovery.

By night, they shared private time together, gradually becoming reacquainted, or perhaps truly acquainted for the first time. The shadows of distrust lingered a while, but eventually yielded to the magnetism between them. Terra held back her longing for a fortnight before succumbing to Connor's embrace. It was his tender response to the first visible sign of the child growing in her womb that tipped the balance. As the palm of his hand passed gently over her softly rounded belly, she allowed it to continue down between her thighs. With her heightened sensuality, she thrilled to his touch, and the last traces of ice melted from her heart.

31

THE PEACEFULNESS of their new life together came to an abrupt end nearly a month after her arrival at Mandala. Late one afternoon, an alarm passed among the populace and made its way to Connor and Terra that intruders had entered the compound. They'd identified themselves as detectives in search of an escaped murderer. They'd tracked him to their compound after months on the run and were now there to arrest him. They had reason to believe that he was in the company of a woman whom they now considered an accomplice.

While Lily held the intruders off at the gates of the compound, Terra and Connor were spirited to a cottage at the far end of the stockade. A jute carpet covering the floor was rolled back, exposing a trap door about the size of a coffin lid. Beneath it was a rectangular space just a few feet deep and large enough for them to fit in close embrace. Two rows of holes along the sides ventilated the space with fresh air blown in from another hidden compartment. As the cover was lowered over the space, they were told that there would be enough air for the next two hours. Lily would do her best to get rid of the intruders by then.

In the darkness of their cramped hideaway, Terra found comfort in the scent of Connor's skin and the warmth of his breath on her face. She was unafraid, ready to die in the arms of her lover. Her only regret if she were to die was for the life growing within her. She would hold on as long as possible for the sake of her child. Her acceptance of the possibility that she might die with Connor renewed her resolve for them to be together if they survived their confinement. In their shared peril, she found the forgiveness she needed to let him fully back into her life.

There was so much she wanted to tell him, but it would have to wait. She wouldn't waste any of their limited air supply on words. She quieted her mind. Her breathing settled into a slow, regular rhythm, which synchronized with Connor's breaths. They became as one.

The time crept by. She had no way to gauge how much time was passing, how much they had left. After a while, the air around them felt thinner and she lingered at the edge of consciousness.

Suddenly, she was back in the cavernous bedroom of Petra's mansion, lying next to her sleeping husband, breathing shallowly. With each breath she felt stabbing pain toward the lower margin of her ribcage near her breastbone on the left and a little lower in her back next to her spine. Her cheek throbbed with pain just below her left eye.

She crept from the bed to retrieve from a hiding place a small glass vial of clear liquid. She broke open the vial at its neck and returned to the bedside. Kresky's right arm lay by his side outside the covers, palm up, exposing the small transdermal window that he'd created in order to efficiently absorb directly into his bloodstream the various nutrients he relied on daily to keep his body young and healthy.

Petra had watched his daily ritual of filling the vessel of the transdermal delivery system with his special concoction and applying it to the window. Now she held the vessel in her left hand and with her right hand tipped the contents of the vial into it. Then she applied it to the window.

In seconds, Kresky's eyes opened wide and stared directly into hers. But he did not move a muscle. His breathing stopped. She felt the corners of her mouth turn up into a smile.

"It ends here, dear Arlo," she said. "You will not hurt me ever again. My punishment is over and this is yours, being able to see me and to hear me and knowing that you will never again draw another breath." She placed two fingers on his carotid artery and waited until there were no more pulsations, then closed his eyes.

As she left the bedside, she heard footsteps, then rustling, followed by a low rumble. She was back in darkness. The pain was gone, but her breathing was still shallow and the air stifling. Then light filtered around the edges of the compartment's lid, accompanied by a rush of fresh air. The lid was shoved aside. Lily and a half dozen other people stood above them. Two teams of three extracted them from the hole and laid them on the floor.

Terra took several gasping breaths and looked over at Connor. He was still and was not breathing. One of the rescuers covered Connor's mouth with his and breathed into his lungs while another applied rhythmic pressure to his chest. Terra watched in suspense. Was she now going to lose him having just decided that she wanted to spend the rest of her life with him? She thought for a moment that it would have been better had they died together. But then, there was her baby, their baby.

His chest heaved with a massive gasp. He was breathing on his own. His eyes were still closed, but he was breathing. His helplessness brought back visions of how she'd cared for him when he'd first returned from his captivity in Ganymede. She felt tears running down her cheeks. He wasn't out of the woods yet, but at least there was hope.

While Connor was moved to the compound's infirmary, Lily filled Terra in on what had transpired aboveground while they were hiding. The intruders, who she suspected were actually bounty hunters, had made a thorough search of the compound and hadn't stumbled upon their tiny vault. Although they'd found nothing, they weren't satisfied that Connor wasn't there. They planned to stake out the compound day and night, watching everyone who entered and left. And they might enter to search again without warning.

"Did he do it?" Lily asked abruptly, taking Terra by the hands. "Did Connor commit that murder?"

Terra looked at her, wondering how much it was prudent to tell.

"No," she replied. "I'm pretty sure he's innocent. But I don't think he has any way to prove it. What do we do now? We can't keep him hidden forever."

"Let's just hope he wakes up," Lily said. "Then we'll worry about dealing with the law."

32

TERRA SAT VIGIL by Connor's bedside for the next twenty-four hours, drinking coffee to stay awake and holding his hand. Just as she was about to succumb to sleep, he opened his eyes. She felt tears well up in the corners of her eyes.

"Don't try to talk," she said, placing a finger on his lips. He kissed her finger and smiled.

She brought him some water and held it to his lips to sip. He took a small sip, licked his lips, then a longer one, and settled back on the pillow.

"I guess we made it," he said.

"You made it by a whisker," she replied. "I thought we'd lost you."

"Not a chance. Not after all we've been through." He paused. "I had the strangest dream."

"Me, too. What was yours?"

"I was back in Petra's bedroom. Not exactly back, but as if I was watching from behind a veil." He paused again. "This is going to sound crazy. Maybe I shouldn't tell you."

"Please...go on," she urged. "What did you see?"

"I saw her sitting by the bed. He was lying in it, asleep. Then she poured something from a vial into some sort of vessel and placed it on his arm." He shook his head. "She was saying something to him. I couldn't see her face, but I could see his eyes. He looked terrified, but he wasn't moving." He paused again. "Terra, I think she killed him."

Terra was astounded at the fidelity of their apparently shared vision. She'd assumed that her flashback had been triggered by the combination of her compromised consciousness and the reminder that the detectives raised of Kresky's unsolved murder. She'd emerged from the vision convinced that it was a memory and not a dream. But how Connor wound up tapping into her experience was a mystery. Perhaps it arose out of the combination of their shared peril and close proximity. Perhaps for him it was a near death experience that provided a moment of omniscience.

"I think she did, too," she said. "It answers a lot. But it doesn't solve your legal problems. The detectives from Boston have pulled back for the moment, but they're not going away. They could be back at any time."

"The baby. What about the baby?" was Connor's next concern.

"It's OK," Terra said. "I got a thorough checkup and there's no evidence that it was harmed. It's heartbeat is strong."

Ordinarily, a period of maternal asphyxia would compromise a pregnancy, likely even end it. But Terra knew that her child was special. Half of its genes carried the Ambrosia Conversion. Like Terra, her child would be likely to enjoy extraordinary robustness, including swift recovery from injury or illness. It was likely the Conversion that had given Terra an advantage over Connor in surviving their underground ordeal.

"Thank God," said Connor, patting her belly. "I'm looking forward to becoming a father."

Another day and Connor was back to full strength and itching to be active. Lily had warned him to lie low as long as the lawmen were still outside their gates, but he could only stay cooped up for so long. The stockade walls provided privacy from prying eyes. An hour or two in the fields couldn't hurt.

"Be careful," Terra cautioned as he headed out after breakfast together. "Don't stay out too long."

Terra was reading in a rocking chair on the porch of their cottage when she heard shrieks of panic from the direction of the pastures. She jumped up and ran in the direction of the screams. A field hand came running from the opposite direction.

"It's Connor," said the field hand, breathless. "He's gone berserk."

Terra kept running until the pasture came into view. There was carnage as far as the eye could see...at least a dozen bodies on the ground. Blood everywhere. People screaming and running in all directions.

At the center of it all was Connor, wielding a machete, swinging it wildly from side to side, cutting down anyone in his path. Sharpshooters came down from the bulwarks, running toward the action, but stopped short when they saw it was Connor. As horrendous as his behavior was, he was still their revered leader. They couldn't bring themselves to pull the trigger.

By the time Terra reached the pasture, the surviving field hands had scattered and Connor stood alone in the center of a paddock menacing with the machete in all directions. Terra picked up a shovel in both hands and headed straight for him. As she got closer, his eyes glowed with hatred and he came at her, brandishing the machete over his head.

"I've got you at last," he sneered, bringing the weapon down toward her head. "It's time for revenge."

Terra parried with the handle of the shovel, blocking the blow. But Connor rained blow after blow until she stumbled and fell to the ground. He was upon her in an instant, the blade pressing against her neck, rage burning in his eyes.

"Ethan!" she exclaimed.

"That's right," he replied with a wicked grin. "I told you we'd meet again. I'm glad you got to see who killed you."

Her hands were against his arms, struggling to hold back the blade. He pressed it harder against her neck. She felt the sharp edge piercing her skin.

The crack of a gunshot rang out and Terra's face was splattered with blood. She felt the pressure of the blade give way. Then he collapsed in a heap on top of her. She rolled his body to the ground and looked in the direction from which the shot had come. There was Lily, smoke coming from the barrel of the rifle she held. Her mouth was set in a straight line. The full horror of what she'd done hadn't yet caught up with her.

Terra looked at what was left of the face of the man she'd adored. It had been blown mostly off, an instant death. Her eyes went to the shoulder wound that was now fully healed. She dug at it with the tip of the machete and probed it with a finger. The tip of her finger found what she was looking for, a round object the size of a pea...the transducer. She dug it out with her finger and found it wrapped with a material that had largely dissolved, a shield that had concealed the device from detection by her scan, and had degraded with time until the transducer was back in contact with Ganymede and with its counterpart implanted in Ethan's last incarnation.

She was still holding the transducer when Lily reached her. She held it out for Lily to see.

"It wasn't Connor," she said. "If you hadn't stopped him, he'd have killed me, then probably dozens of others. He was bent on destroying this place."

"I know, Darlin'. I figured it out. How do you think I could do what I just did?" She looked down at her son's body and ran her fingers through his matted hair. It wasn't Connor, but it wasn't Ethan anymore either. Then she looked at Terra with an expression that told Terra that they were thinking the same thing.

"Then what's become of my boy?" she asked. "Where do we find Connor?"

"Back at Ganymede," Terra said. "If he's alive, he's their prisoner again. It seems we're back where we started."

33

IT HAD BEEN THE WORST day that the people of Mandala had ever experienced. By the time it ended, Ethan had killed eleven members of their community and maimed another dozen. Their first priority was tending to the wounded. Then they would deal with the dead, including Connor's body.

There was still the matter of the men who'd come to Mandala to arrest Connor. The sounds of the ruckus hadn't escaped their notice. Once it was over, they were back at the gates demanding to be let inside.

Terra saw an opportunity arise out of all the chaos and destruction. If they'd come for Connor, then they could have him. She and Lily were both willing to part with his body if it would put the manhunt to rest once and for all. Terra carefully shaved a thin layer from the tip of Connor's left ring finger and pressed it between thin sheets of carbon fiber, then slipped into the shadows while others drew open the gates and invited the lawmen in. Once inside, they could see the carnage still on the ground.

One of them let out a long whistle. "What the hell happened here?" he demanded.

"You were right," said one of the villagers. "The man you were after was hiding here, and when we found him, he went berserk and began killing everyone in sight. Our leader shot him dead. There's his body." He pointed to the corpse now wrapped in a shroud except for his head. The visitors could see clearly that he was dead, but there was too little left of his face to identify him.

It took less than an hour for them to perform a forensic examination of the body and to confirm via fingerprints and DNA that it was their fugitive. They insisted on bringing him back to their jurisdiction so that they could close their case. From the mayhem they'd just witnessed, he was clearly a ruthless killer, leaving no doubt that he was responsible for the death of Arlo Kresky.

Lily approached them as they prepared to leave.

"Please give us some time before you break the story so that we can bury our dead before the media descends on us. We need time to pay our respects in peace."

"Don't worry, lady," replied one of the men, "He'll be worth just as much in the morning."

"Bounty hunters, after all," thought Terra as she listened from the wings. "No better than vultures."

Terra had coached Lily about asking the men to withhold their story. Once Ganymede figured out that Ethan had been killed, they'd have no further reason to keep Connor alive. It would still be only a matter of hours before Ethan would be missed. Meanwhile, Terra had a sample of a fingerprint and DNA from Connor's body, which Ganymede now believed belonged to Ethan, and the transducer she'd recovered from the wound. Ganymede's security depended upon redundant verification. Its agents' transducers had long been used as one of their credentials for gaining admittance to their stations. Terra secured the transducer to the neck of one of Lily's trusted aides so that it would keep moving while Ganymede tracked it, maintaining the illusion that Ethan was still alive.

The next task was to identify the man in whose body Connor now presumably resided. Should they succeed in breaching

Ganymede's defenses, they'd need to find him fast, make a positive identification, and separate him from the others. Terra generated a sufficiently detailed portrait from memory to run through facial recognition. He was identified as Tobias Batie, a former lumberjack from Tennessee who'd come into sudden wealth years before and built a construction empire. A current scan of the UDB found that Batie had disappeared suddenly five and a half weeks before, around the same time that Lily shot Ethan the first time on the outskirts of Mandala.

The FBI had spearheaded a search for Batie, but could find no trace. The missing person information was shared among public law enforcement and all the covert agencies of the government. This was a stroke of luck that Terra could use in her plan to raid Ganymede and rescue Connor. Her former section chief at the NSA before she was recruited away to Ganymede had advanced through the ranks to a position near the top of the command. She'd reach out to him for help. Hopefully he'd remember her and take her message seriously. She composed a brief missive to send via an encrypted channel they'd used years ago to communicate with one another.

"Quentin," the message began. "I know who took Tobias Batie and where they are holding him. They are the same people responsible for the mind swapping conspiracy that broke last month. I think I can gain access to their base, but I'll need backup. Please send a special ops team to meet me at 1500 hours at the coordinates that follow this message. Please instruct them that the occupants must be taken alive. Terra."

Terra retrieved the transducer from Lily's aide, tucked it in her waistband along with Connor's fingerprint, and headed back to DC. The car let her out a quarter mile from the entrance to Ganymede's tunnel at 2:45. She slipped toward the entrance and prayed for the arrival of Quentin's force. Thanks to the Director, she now had porcelain toned skin to complement her trademark red hair by which Quentin would instruct the NSA team to recognize her.

The cars rolled up at 2:59 and two dozen agents fanned out around the hidden entrance to the tunnel, the coordinates that Terra had provided. Terra came out of hiding and led them into the tunnel to the entry portal. She took a deep breath, withdrew the carbon fiber packet from her waistband, and applied the fingertip to the sensor on the portal. The system, if it worked as she remembered, would pick up the signal from the transducer automatically. She held her breath. Twenty seconds passed. Nothing happened.

Then she heard the whirring of a lock and the portal swung open. The crack team rushed into the void in pairs, capturing each of the ten Ganymede agents without firing a shot. Terra spotted Connor bound to a chair and freed him just as an NSA operative escorted the Director from his inner office.

Terra's eyes went first to the Director's hands, which was the only way she knew for sure how to identify him. Then she saw his face in the light for the first time. He was far older looking than she'd even imagined. His cheeks sagged in jowls that together with the bags under his eyes made him look something like an ancient basset hound. His eyelids sagged, half covering irises ringed in gray circles, another mark of his advanced age. He was also smaller than she'd imagined. He looked impotent and defenseless.

Their eyes met. Then suddenly he smiled and winked at her. She saw the muscles of his jaw tense as he bit down on something and collapsed in a heap on the ground. All around the enclosure, captured Ganymede agents collapsed to the ground. Within seconds they were all dead. Only Terra understood the terrible significance of what she'd just observed.

Terra took advantage of the confusion to slip out through the portal with Connor. Once in the open they broke into a run and were soon out of sight. Since Tobias Batie had undergone the Ambrosia Conversion, Connor now enjoyed all the same physical advantages that Terra did and easily kept up with her. They eluded the NSA team with ease.

On the way back to Mandala, Terra tried to prepare Connor for what he was about to find. He'd understood that Ethan had switch places with him, but had no idea what he'd planned to do once that occurred. Nothing she could tell him, however, would protect him from the full impact of the loss he was about to face.

When they arrived back at Mandala the community was deeply engrossed in dealing with the dead. They'd resurrected the long-abandoned tradition of burial in keeping with their belief in the cycle of life and the return of human remains to the earth from which they had come. Since embalming poisoned the ground and prevented bodies from decomposing, they buried their dead unembalmed in simple shrouds, which made it imperative for burial to be done promptly.

Connor dealt with his grief by throwing himself into the task of tending to the dead. With his superhuman strength and the intensity of his emotions, he dug most of the graves singlehandedly. He knelt beside each body, touching each face tenderly and whispering to each of his fallen brethren before committing them to the earth.

By the time they got to bed that night, they were both emotionally and physically spent. They fell asleep side by side without anything left to consider the question that hung over them from the moment they reunited inside Ganymede. Would they still want to be together?

34

CONNOR SAT BY TERRA'S BEDSIDE as she held her swaddled newborn daughter to her breast. The child was strikingly beautiful, with Connor's blue eyes and Petra's olive skin. Even if they hadn't mapped her genes, there would have been no doubt about her parentage.

Following the raid on Ganymede, it was no longer safe for their community to remain at Mandala. Its location had become known to Ganymede. At some point the Director would assemble his followers and attempt to resurrect his organization. He would likely come after Terra who would be the single most critical threat to the secrecy of his survival. And Terra had no way to know in what physical form they might eventually appear. While Ganymede no longer had its infrastructure, in some ways its threat was more insidious than ever.

Under Connor's guidance, Mandala picked up stakes within forty-eight hours and was in search of a new place to plant their extended family where it might thrive. With the collapse of Ganymede, they no longer pursued a mission beyond the boundaries of their community. They were free, at least for now, to embrace the essence of their philosophy and to integrate their lives with the natural environment.

Terra and Lily had scanned the map for a suitable place to put down new roots. Oregon's Willamette Valley had once been home to some of the most fertile farmlands on the continent before it was wiped out by an environmental catastrophe in the mid-thirties. The valley had long since recovered its lushness, but had not been heavily repopulated, presenting an ideal combination of rich soil, abundant water, and a cloak of anonymity. The community of Mandala took its place among a scattering of family farms in a remote part of the valley.

Since they'd left behind the technological trappings of their former quest, their presence in their new home and the history of their community remained obscure. Their neighbors saw them only as kindred spirits. Terra had little interest in tangling with Ganymede again and hoped that they could live under the radar indefinitely.

Once the dust had settled from their ordeal, Terra discovered that her feelings for Connor transcended her attraction to his body. Her passion was soon rekindled with the new Connor. Fortunately, Tobias Batie had been wired for heterosexuality and the passion was mutual. There was still much to be forgiven between them, but their bond proved strong enough to weather the challenge.

Terra also had much for which to forgive herself. She hoped that she could live a life that honored the person in whose body she now lived.

The door to the room opened and Lily entered. She embraced her son, then turned to Terra and smiled. The twinkle had returned to her eye. She asked if she could hold her grandchild. Terra handed her over.

"She's gorgeous," Lily said. "Have you decided what to name her?"

"Yes," she said, looking at Connor, "We've decided to call her Macklyn."

About the Author

Rick Moskovitz is a Harvard educated psychiatrist who taught psychotherapy and spent nearly four decades listening to his patients tell their stories. After leaving practice, he in turn became a storyteller, writing science fiction that explores the psychological consequences of living in a world of expanding possibilities, including even the prospect of evading death. His characters deal with enduring moral and emotional struggles against a backdrop of a near future world that is still dealing with environmental crises as it navigates the intersection of human and artificial intelligence.

www.ingramcontent.com/pod-product-compliance
Lightning Source LLC
Chambersburg PA
CBHW070928130626
46555CB00001B/330